Poems From Across The UK & Overseas

Edited by Vivien Linton

First published in Great Britain in 2009 by

YoungWriters

Remus House
Coltsfoot Drive
Peterborough
PE2 9JX
Telephone: 01733 890066
Website: www.youngwriters.co.uk

Book Design by Spencer Hart

SB ISBN 978-1-84924-487-9

Foreword

At Young Writers our defining aim is to promote an enjoyment of reading and writing amongst children and young adults. By giving aspiring poets the opportunity to see their work in print, their love of the written word as well as confidence in their own abilities has the chance to blossom.

Our latest competition Poetry Explorers was designed to introduce primary school children to the wonders of creative expression. They were given free reign to write on any theme and in any style, thus encouraging them to use and explore a variety of different poetic forms.

We are proud to present the resulting collection of regional anthologies which are an excellent showcase of young writing talent. With such a diverse range of entries received, the selection process was difficult yet very rewarding. From comical rhymes to poignant verses, there is plenty to entertain and inspire within these pages. We hope you agree that this collection bursting with imagination is one to treasure.

Contents

All Saints CE Primary School, Nuneaton

Corey Cousins 1
Kerry Daffern 1

Archibald First School, Newcastle upon Tyne

Ryan Stokes (8) 1
Elliott Groves (9) 2
Hannah Wilson (8) 3
Olivia Corrigan (9) 4
Zain Khan (9) 5
Ellice Moran (9) 6
Tom Smith (8) 6
Euan Wyatt (9) 7
Georgia Thursby (9) 7
James Boothroyd (9) 7

Ashurst CE VA Primary School, Steyning

Rebecca Loveless (10) 8
Dominic Hill (11) 9
Kieran Fogarty (9) 9
Harriet Shoosmith (10) 10
Joel Northam (11) 10
Nicholas van Pelt (10) 11
Harriet Middleton (10) 11
Hamish Garnett (11) 12
William Bridger (11) 12
Amalie Meldrum (10) 13
Natalie Ford (10) 13
Archie Croft (10) 14
Owen Mattia (10) 15
Charlie Treasure (10) 16

British International School of Stavanger, Stavanger, Norway

Libby Anne Taylor (10) 16
Rebecca Waller (10) 17
Havana Coleman-Wood (10) 17
Steven Ediriweera ((10) 18
Olivia Churchfield (10) 18
Siddesh Pachkawade (9) 18
Tom Beeley (9) 19
Hazel Highton (9) 19
Joshua King-Batsios 19
Alisha Haroon (10) 20
Nifemi Adeogba (9) 20
Konrad Gjerstad (9) 20
Oliver Lee (9) 21
Daniel James Sayer (10) 21
Louis Arkwright (10) 21

Lawmuir Primary School, Bellshill

Marcus Hickson 21
Hayley McCall 22
Adam Brown 22
Thomas Aagesen (8) 22
Nickolas McInally 23
Lauren Quinn (9) 23
Josh Thompson 23
Stephen Crombie 24
Siobhan Donald (8) 24
David Gault (8) 24
Rhianna Fowler (7) 25
Marc Shilliday 25
Ross Pender (8) 25
Chloe Hogg (9) 26
Emma Marchbank 26
Kayla Cathcart 26
Cameron McDougall 27
Amy Clemenson (8) 27

Lauren McKellar 27
Oliver Hickson 28
Chloe Clemenson................................. 28

Leighterton Primary School, Tetbury

Hannah Cicely Oliver (10) 29
Polly Webb (10) 30
Charlotte Corderoy (11) 31
Amy Fry (11) 32
Callum Sadler (11) 33
Harry Palmer (10) 33
Ellie Ashley (10) 34
Oliver Osborne (10)............................. 34
Hannah Cook (10)............................... 35
Murray Thomson (11).......................... 35
Adam James Cox (10) 36
Tammie Louise Scrivens (10) &
Melissa Beale (11)............................... 36
Emanuelle Paulson (10) 37

Malvern Parish CE Primary School, Malvern

Stephanie Ruhback (10) 37
Michael Brown (11) 38
Bethany Wolff (9)................................. 38
Joanna Chappell (11)........................... 39
Tyler Bond (11) 39
Chloe Bircham (10) 40
Olivia Rhodes (10)............................... 40
Lois Jones (9)...................................... 41
Emma Bradley (10) 41
Rebecca Wells (10) 42
Andrew Pickering (10) 42
Elizabeth Prior (10).............................. 43
Tobie Timmermans (11) 43
Abigail Morris (9) 44
Josh Walwyn (10) 44
Anna Bradley (10)................................ 45
Katie Reed (11) 45
Maddie Howell (9) 46
Chloe Prince (11)................................. 46
Chloe Buckland (11) 47
Chloe Roberts 47
Sky Pardoe Davies (10)....................... 48
Evan Wyn Jones (10) 48
Nathan Watts (8) 48
Sarah Chappell (9) 49
Amy Griffiths (8)................................... 49
Aletéa Palmer-Price (8)........................ 50
Naomi Chakko-George (7).................. 50
Hannah White (8) 51
Thomas Reed (8) 51
Thomas Baker (7)................................ 52
Adam Sturge (8).................................. 52
James Sheldrake (7) 52
Emily Jane Standen (9) 53
Jacob Chakko-George (9) 53
India Timmermans (9) 53
Ellie Rose Blannin (9) 54
Thomas Prior (8).................................. 54
Natasha Smith (9) 54
Alina Benny (8).................................... 55
Niall Delahunty & Jake May (8) 55
James Howell (8) 55
Natasha Knight (9) 56
Georgina Smith (9).............................. 56
Lee Woolley (7).................................... 56

Moorlands J&I School, West Bromwich

Matthew Hazlehurst (9) 57
Rebecca Tandy (9) 58
Leroy Lokko (9) 58
Millie Boughton (9) 59
Emily Berry (9) 59
Christopher Fullwood (9)...................... 60
Jordan Alexander (9) 60
Lauren Jones (8) 61
Joshua Richardson (9)......................... 61
Chloe Hames (9) 61

Muscat International School, Ruwi, Sultanate of Oman

Shahed Ali Al-Nadabi (11).................... 62
Fatima Hussain (11) 64
Khadija Fardan Al-Hamdany (12) 64
Amna Aftab (11) 66

Yousef Al Riyami (10) 66
Nicole Vacca (11) 67
Sherine Bou Dargham (11) 68
Seif Alhajri (12) 69
Sana Shahid (11) 70
Wasan Al Bulushi (11) 71
Lujainah Talal Saif Al-Subhi (11) 72
Iram Al-Ghafri (12) 73
Azim Baruno (9) 73
Katya Plotnikova (11) 74
Muhammad Naufal (12) 75
Syed Hassan Imam (12) 76
Ruwaid Al Habbi (13) 77
Rifat Hassan (11) 78
Casey Beatson (12) 79
Aimen Haider (11) 80
Assam Munir (12) 81
Haneen Ahmad Rashed Ibrahim (11) 82
Yousuf Al-Mahrooqi (7) 83
Tamima Al Shanfari (9) 83
Malak Al Nadabi (9) 84
Xiao Wensherg Xiao (9) 84
Tegan Al-Harthi (11) 85
Fauzan Nor Azmi (9) 85
Swafiya Sheikh (11) 86
Jasmine Craven (9) 86
Maha Al-Balushi (11) 87
Reem Ali (9) 87
Maha Raya (8) 88
Amira Al Jabri (11) 89
Mudrick Mussa (12) 90
Elay Nasser Mubarak Al-Araimi (10) 91
Azzam Abdullah Ali Al-Nabri (12) 92
Sarosh Shahid Al-Querish (12) 93
Mohammed Hussain Al-Nabhani 94
Ramsha Khalid (11) 95
Mohammed Abdullah Khalid (12) 96
Hind (11) 97
Najla (11) 97
Manal Al Azri (12) 98
Zainah Hassan (11) 99
Mohammed Al-Wahaibi (11) 100
Taimur Fatik Fahar Alsaid (11) 101

Rufford CE Primary School, Ormskirk

Lewis Birch (9) 101
Jim Quinlan (9) 102
Amelia Hickson (10) 102
Jakob Blundell (9) 103
Jack William Onions (9) 103
Michael Golding (10) 104
Matthew Taylor (10) 104
Katie Cottam (9) 105
Joe Skinley (10) 105
Emily Potter (9) 105
Tom Ainscough (9) 106
Lauren Shacklady (10) 106

St Helen Auckland Primary School, Bishop Auckland

Callum Freeman (8) 106
Matthew Tones (9) 107
Joshua Legg (9) 107

St Hilda's CE Primary School, Manchester

Natasher Devlin (11) 108

St Lawrence CE Primary School, Hurstpierpoint

Georgina Easterbrook (10) 109
Harry Young (10) 109
Elliot Barton (10) 110
Barney Dunnett (9) 110
James Syms (10) 111
Jonathan Kemp (11) 111
Joseph Simpson (11) 112
Jemima Edwards (8) 112
Madeleine Madgwick (10) 113
George Disney (8) 113
Benjamin Lynch (8) 114
Oliver Towers (11) 114
Molly Fullard (8) 115
Holly Spencer (11) 115
Harry Forsdick (8) 116
Nadia Bartlett (8) 116

Bethany Wattam (11) 117
Honor Bryant (8) 117
Lauren Finch 118
Brandon Haylor (7) 118
Megan Burholt (9) 119
Reece Piper (9) 119
David Jackson (8) 120
Maya Farlow (11) 120
Rachel Dickinson (10) 120
Joseph Holland-Villa (8) 121
Joshua Hughes (8) 121
Lukas Kemp (9) 121
Matilda Jones (9) 122
Nina Ince (11) 122
Reine Tucker (9) 122
Finn Monteith (9) 123
Chloe Wallis (11) 123
Alex Moulder (9) 123
Jill Sanger (10) 124
Charlotte Ledger (9) 124
Zöe Stevens (11) 124
Charlotte Burholt (11) 125
Rebecca Regan (11) 125

The British School of Amsterdam, Amsterdam, Holland

Moritz von Contzen (11) 125
Natalie Schmit (8) 126
Ashling Martin (9) 126
Ben Graham (10) 127
Eve Turner (9) 127
Cassie Howarth-Knight (10) 128
Lasya Karthikeyan (10) 129
Xavier Raychell (8) 130
Thomas Benjamin Elgar (11) 131
Isobel Anderson (10) 131
Sherien Burger (8) 132
Kalina Milenova (9) 132
Shashank Narayan (11) 133
Kirsty Graham (9) 134

The Highway Primary School, Orpington

Ashley Hill (10) 134
Natasha Fenn &
Francesca Telling (10) 135
Danny Hill (9) & Miles Hughes (10) 135
Scott Simner (10) 135
Rebecca Fryza (10) 136

Welbeck Primary School, Newcastle upon Tyne

Sarah Louise Davidson (10) 136
Aimee Cowan (7) 137
Charlotte Anne Haigh (8) 137
Annie Mbikayi (8) 138
Tanya Zengenene (8) 138
John-Paul Goossens (7) 138
Jamie Brushfield (10) 139
Katie Chat (8) 139

West Park Middle School, Worthing

Helen Skingley (10) 140

Wilton Primary School, Hawick

Rian Taylor (11) 140
Erin Craig (11) 141
Shannon Scott (11) 141
Ella Cairns (11) 142
Mathew King (10) 142
Kirsten Scott (11) 143
Charlotte Dickens (10) 143
Georgia Kirkpatrick (10) 144
Madeleine Irvine (10) 144
Liam Smith (10) 145
Cristina Antonacci (10) 145
Shannon Gullen (11) 145
Connor Smith (10) 146
Kasey Watson (11) 146
Ailsa Nairn (11) 147
Michael Smyth (10) 147

The Poems

Laughter

Laughter sounds like fun
Laughter tastes like a cherry bun
Laughter smells like fresh air
Laughter looks like children
Having fun at the fair
Laughter feels like an exploding
Water bomb
Laughter reminds me of my celebrity mates,
Dick and Dom.

Corey Cousins
All Saints CE Primary School, Nuneaton

Fun

Fun sounds like children laughing,
Fun tastes like pink candyfloss,
Fun smells like bubbles blowing in the breeze,
Fun looks like flying kites over trees,
Fun feels soft and fluffy,
Fun reminds me of my family.
Fun, fun, fun!

Kerry Daffern
All Saints CE Primary School, Nuneaton

Acrostic

A crostic poems are really cool to do
C reepy, funny poems to see
R eally good types of poems like scary poems
O r friendly poems
S ome poems can rhyme some don't
T ic toc poems about the clock
I t might be rubbish it might be good
C os this is the end, and goodbye.

Ryan Stokes (8)
Archibald First School, Newcastle upon Tyne

Autumn

Autumn is red,
Autumn is yellow,
Autumn has conkers that fall
To the floor.

Autumn is brown,
Autumn is orange,
Autumn has trees that sway
In the breeze.

Autumn is green,
Autumn is pink,
Autumn has nights that are as
Cold as a freezer.

Autumn is happy,
Autumn is joyful,
Autumn has Hallowe'en that
Scares all the neighbours.

Autumn is loud,
Autumn is quiet,
Autumn has fireworks that
Light up the sky.

Autumn is gentle,
Autumn is fun,
Autumn has frost that patrols
The night's darkness.

Autumn is great,
Autumn is wonderful,
Autumn is the greatest season
Of all.

Elliott Groves (9)
Archibald First School, Newcastle upon Tyne

Habits Poem

A is for Alex, who is a superstar
B is for Ben, who has a massive car
C is for Chris, who has a long tail
D is for Dan, who bites his nails
E is for Ellie, who swallows her gum
F is for Fay, who has a big bum
G is for Georgia, who has some great books
H is for Harry, who plays with black hooks
I is for Ivan, who wears a pink wig
J is for Jack, who eats like a pig
K is for Keiron, who picks his nose
L is for Lyla, who drinks from a hose
M is for Matt, who thinks he's the best
N is for Nicola, who is a real pest
O is for Olivia, who is my friend
P is for Pat, who drives me round the bend
Q is for Quincy, who loves his name
R is for Rebecca, with a dog who is very tame
S is for Sarah, who wants to be in a band
T is for Tim, who owns lots of land
U is for Una, who loves to eat donuts
V is for Verity, who loves to eat nuts
W is for Will, who eats lots of sweets
X is for Xanthe, who has lots of treats
Y is for Yen, who always bumps his head
Z is for Zain, who lies in his shed.

Hannah Wilson (8)
Archibald First School, Newcastle upon Tyne

Habits Poem

A is for Alex, who bites all her nails
B is for Billy, who wags all his tails
C is for Carol, who swallows her gum
D is for David, who can be quite dumb
E is for Edward, who wears a grey wig
F is for Fay, who eats like a pig
G is for Garry, who has hair like green grass
H is for Hannah, who likes to do Mass
I is for Ian, who is always so sad
J is for Jackie, who's always been bad
K is for Katy, who has some great styles
L is for Layla, who has lots of piles
M is Mary, who calls herself Pat
N is for Neena, who wears a pink hat
O is for Ollie, who walks in the dark
P is for Patrick, the dog who won't bark
Q is for Queeny, who quits all her jobs
R is for Rachel, who will always sob
S is for Sam, who acts like an ape
T is for Tim, who wastes Sellotape
U is for Umar, who steals lots of money
V is for Vera, who thinks she's so funny
W is for William, who wears an earring
X is for Xavia, who will always sing
Y is for Yen, who always falls over
Z is for Zain, who likes Pavlova.

Olivia Corrigan (9)
Archibald First School, Newcastle upon Tyne

Food

A is for apricots juicy and sweet
B is for bacon, which goes good with meat.
C is for carrots, a very nice food
D is for doughnuts, they put you in a mood.
E is for eggs with the yellow yolk
F is for fish, I say to my folk.
G is for grapes, juicy and red
H is for Haribos, they're under my bed.
I is for ice cream, icy like anything
J is for jam, eaten by the king.
K is for kiwi fruit, spiky and rough,
L is for lemon, gone in a puff.
M is for melon, full of seeds
N is for nachos, which is a good feed.
O is for orange, smells of feet
P is for pear, tastes bad with meat.
Q is for Quavers, crisp 'n' green
R is for radish, smooth and clean.
S is for sweetcorn, sweet and smooth
T is for turnip, can on the move.
U is for ugli fruit, its name is right!
V is for vegetables, some you bite.
W is for whiskers, the disgusting cat food
Xtra strong mints they get you out a mood.
Y is for yoghurt, creamy and cool
Z is for zest, eat that you're a fool!

Zain Khan (9)
Archibald First School, Newcastle upon Tyne

I Wanna

I wanna be a superstar
I wanna be a pop princess
I wanna join the famous crew
I wanna have some shoes so new
I wanna have some limousines
I wanna be in magazines
I wanna take some dancing classes
I wanna wear some funky glasses
I wanna have a microphone
I wanna have a dog to own
I wanna be in royalty,
I wanna meet the majesty.

Ellice Moran (9)
Archibald First School, Newcastle upon Tyne

My Bike, Pasta – Haikus

My Bike

My muddy black bike
From lots of races, of course
A good thing for me.

Pasta

Food from Italy
My favourite thing to eat
A bowl of pasta.

Tom Smith (8)
Archibald First School, Newcastle upon Tyne

Superstar

I wanna be a superstar
I wanna have a pet jaguar
I wanna have a rich wife
I wanna have different life
I wanna live in New York
I wanna live on pure pork
I wanna lot of caviar
I wanna be a superstar!

Euan Wyatt (9)
Archibald First School, Newcastle upon Tyne

Friends

F riends are really important to have
R eally fun to play with
I ncredible, oh yes they are
E asy to find they sometimes are
N ice ones are better than horrible ones
D oing fun things together.
S illy sometimes, but that's what friends are.

Georgia Thursby (9)
Archibald First School, Newcastle upon Tyne

Friends

F riends are good to have
R yan and Ewan are my friends
I have lots of nice friends in my class
E veryone is my friend
N ever trust people who aren't your friends
D o play with your friends
S uper friends are my friends.

James Boothroyd (9)
Archibald First School, Newcastle upon Tyne

Planet Rap

You cannot live on Mercury
It's simply far too hot.
If you went too near you would
Burn a lot.

Venus is the second planet,
With no moon,
With volcanoes about to
Erupt soon.

Earth is the third planet from
The sun,
If you live there you're
Sure to have fun.

Mars is a planet,
Browny red,
And it would blow away
Your bed.

In the solar system, Jupiter
Is big,
And is ginormous compared
With a fig.

Uranus is made of methane
Gas,
With a wind travelling
At mass.

Neptune is a dark planet,
Far away,
And you couldn't see
Aliens play.

Pluto is the smallest, and
Last of all,
So small it looks like a
Tennis ball.

Rebecca Loveless (10)
Ashurst CE VA Primary School, Steyning

The Four Stages Of Life

Babyhood is spring,
A fresh and new beginning
Flowers, trees and shrubs
Coming up and begging for light.

Childhood is summer, clear and happy,
All plants are growing tall and proud.
But their quest for light is over,
Flowers, trees and shrubs are growing
And the sun's like an everlasting light.

Adulthood is autumn, like a tree losing its leaves
As it gets older it grows moss and fungi,
The leaves are getting crippled like a goldy-brown colour
And every day through autumn the
Flowers, trees and shrubs also get brown and shrivelled.

Old age is winter, dull and dark
Snow floating down with no control.
And as the winter passes
All the flowers, trees and shrubs are dying
And enjoying their last few breaths.

Dominic Hill (11)
Ashurst CE VA Primary School, Steyning

Spring

Spring is a parcel, wrapped with a blazing heat and
Shining meadows with bright hopes flying by

Spring is a parcel with colourful flowers, one blazing red,
One bright yellow, forming a pattern

Spring is a parcel, a warm breeze
Unwrapping the parcel before my eyes

Spring is a parcel, unleashing a baking heat
Being held up high.

Kieran Fogarty (9)
Ashurst CE VA Primary School, Steyning

The Four Stages Of Life

Infancy is a yearling, lively and determined,
Its eyes wandering and learning constantly,
Gathering his balance and falling again and again,
Busy till the day ends, and when the sun creeps behind the clouds.

Childhood is a beaver, fun and energetic,
Eating and gnawing at all things possible,
Using every hour possible to play and do as little work,
Social hours used playing with friends.

Adulthood is a bumblebee,
Patient and hungry, providing for its family,
Busy and tired, but never gives up,
He helpfully wanders from flower to flower,
Waiting for the end of his busy day.

Old age is a tortoise, slow and kind,
Stumbling across the sand, quiet and fearless,
Watching over the other tortoises, he dreams all day,
Remembering when he was once that age.

Harriet Shoosmith (10)
Ashurst CE VA Primary School, Steyning

January Cinquains

Rainfall
Drizzling down fast,
Patt'ring, clatt'ring, soaking,
People running to their dry house,
Rainy.

The wind
Howling, screaming,
Whining, rushing, storming,
Flying down, pandemonium,
Crashing.

Joel Northam (11)
Ashurst CE VA Primary School, Steyning

The Four Stages Of Life

Infancy is a sunny day
With the sound of a young bird tweeting
In the top of a small birch tree
Waiting for its mother to come back with lunch.

Childhood is a bouncing kangaroo
Leaping around an enclosure at the zoo
Learning about the outside world
Waiting for play.

Adulthood is a prowling lion
Finding food for its family
Its mane golden with a tint of silver
Scared of getting old and brittle.

Old age is a wise owl
With a ton of fun
With a glimpse of silver feathers
Happily perched on a closely set branch.

Nicholas van Pelt (10)
Ashurst CE VA Primary School, Steyning

Spring Is A Parcel!

Spring is a parcel, its yellow, crinkly paper,
Being so perfect, but not quite as great as summer.

Spring is a parcel, tied up with all sorts of bright,
Bouncy flowers,
And relieving us from the cold, icy cruelty of winter.

Spring is a parcel, the light, fragile breeze tickling the
Delicate paper and almost revealing its colourful contents.

Spring is a parcel, the cold hands of winter stiffly
Reaching down
And finally giving us the happiness of lambs and
Glowing flowers.

Harriet Middleton (10)
Ashurst CE VA Primary School, Steyning

The Four Stages Of Life

Babyhood is an expanding root,
Small and ready to get up,
Reaching out for its food,
Standing steady.

Childhood is a young leopard,
Ready and active,
Pouncing on its food,
Finding its future.

Adulthood is a huge elephant,
Standing proud,
Feeling very tough,
Watching over his family very carefully.

Old age is a tortoise,
Thinking about its past,
Shrinking and getting weaker,
Resting for ever.

Hamish Garnett (11)
Ashurst CE VA Primary School, Steyning

Spring

Spring is a parcel, sunny and bright
Sun so bright it blinds you, so hot it burns you

Spring is a parcel, shining in the rain
The colours of the rainbow come and stay

Spring is a parcel, the little blue tits open up
The people who see, gasp and wrap it back up

Spring is a parcel, the people who see
See a little baby rocking in a cot.

William Bridger (11)
Ashurst CE VA Primary School, Steyning

The Four Stages Of Life

Babyhood is a small drop of water
Innocent and powerless
Reaching out and crying for Mum
Finally, tired, it lies down to sleep.

Childhood is a busy thrush
Quick and bouncy
Learning about new things
Pecking frantically at its food.

Adulthood is a fast cheetah
Busy and protective
Working hard to find her food
Cleaning her young carefully.

Old age is a slow tortoise
Steadily taking its time
Never rushing, always friendly
Sitting down and falling into a never-ending sleep.

Amalie Meldrum (10)
Ashurst CE VA Primary School, Steyning

Spring's Gift

Spring is a parcel, wrapped in mazes of green
With luscious forests opening up the gateways.

Spring is a parcel with the reeds of the waters
Soon joined together, a symbol of friendship.

Spring is a parcel, the breeze and warmth opens
And reveals a pathway with bubbling streams.

Spring is a parcel with a gift of new life
Swifting and swaying with the wind.

Natalie Ford (10)
Ashurst CE VA Primary School, Steyning

The Four Stages Of Life

Infancy is a young, playful dolphin,
Shedding light on the dark, misty water
Squeaking as it jumps with joy,
Learning intently as it goes.

Childhood is a young zebra,
Running with its herd,
Becoming unique and special,
In its own way.

Adulthood is a strong lion,
More powerful each day,
King of the jungle,
Majestic in all ways.

Old age is a slow cat,
Mournfully limping to its bed,
Gaining wisdom as he goes,
Sharing all in his time.

Archie Croft (10)
Ashurst CE VA Primary School, Steyning

The Four Stages Of Life

Infancy is a baby kangaroo
Hopping around the outback
Having full protection in his mother's pouch
It's like a shield.

Childhood is a young lion
Learning how to stalk his prey
Teeth growing, getting stronger
Finally going to find a pride.

Adulthood is a hedgehog
After a while his spikes hardening up
To make full protection
Eventually having children of his own.

Old age is a tortoise
Elderly and frail
Slow and clever
Calmly chomping on his food.

Owen Mattia (10)
Ashurst CE VA Primary School, Steyning

The Four Stages Of Life

Infancy is a baby monkey
With his mum helping him jump from tree to tree
Waiting for her to gather up leaves for them to eat
Playing play-fighting with fellow friends.

Childhood is a monkey playing in the trees with his friend
Jumping to get the best leaves on different trees
Trying to get the most leaves
And seeing who can finish them first.

Adulthood is a monkey which is responsible for its children
Protecting them from their predators
It's also about making the right decisions and
The most safe ones.

Old age is an ancient sofa
Getting sat on by new cushions
Gathering dust as it travels
Around the world going to new homes.

Charlie Treasure (10)
Ashurst CE VA Primary School, Steyning

Mother Earth

Every bit of nature counts,
Every tree,
Every flower,
Every strand of grass.

Every bit of pollution,
Is another puzzle piece to the end of the world.

Is this what you want to happen to the Earth?
For it to die with no one pitying it,
For all life to be exterminated?
If not, then,
Do what you can,
Save Mother Earth!

Libby Anne Taylor (10)
British International School of Stavanger, Stavanger, Norway

Lost

Lost in the jungle,
I see the lion coming.
Lost in the jungle,
I hear the monkeys screaming.
Lost in the jungle,
Lost forever
I wish I was in my comfortable bed.

Cannibals dancing, dancing round the fire.
I hope they don't see me.
I hope they don't hear me.
I wish I was in my comfortable bed.

I fly and I fly, with the wind in my hair.
On a pink little cloud, I float in the sky.
I look down to see the things on the ground.
I can't see so much, I'm tired now.
I'm laying down on my pink little cloud
I'm floating away, I'm falling into a dream.

Rebecca Waller (10)
British International School of Stavanger, Stavanger, Norway

In The Jungle!

In the jungle, the brave explorer
Swayed through the jungle
Finding new, exotic things.
Swinging on a tree
Here and there
Looking everywhere
Rattlesnakes and tigers
Monkeys and poisonous spiders
If you get in trouble
There's no way out!

Beware of the jungle!

Havana Coleman-Wood (10)
British International School of Stavanger, Stavanger, Norway

The Hard Things Are The Right Things

Polluting is easy, and doesn't take a lot of muscle,
Maybe that's why people litter,
They can't be bothered to clean up.
Saving the Earth may be hard, but it's the right thing to do.
Isn't it?
Well?
It's not every day you come across somebody picking up litter.
But at least every day you see litter.
Maybe we can change that
And save the world.
That's the right thing, isn't it?

Steven Ediriweera ((10)
British International School of Stavanger, Stavanger, Norway

Exploring

Flying through the clouds
On glorious silver wings
Looking down on Earth
To see all living things.

Spiders crawling up your back
But you don't really think
Then when you see the monster
You run before you blink.

Olivia Churchfield (10)
British International School of Stavanger, Stavanger, Norway

India

I ndia is hot
N ew things happen
D oing lots of work
I play with my friend
A nd at night we talk a lot!

Siddesh Pachkawade (9)
British International School of Stavanger, Stavanger, Norway

My Bed

My bed is dangerous
It's a crocodile's head
My duvet's a car
It's the warty body of
Uncle Bobby.
But that's nothing, until it's a full moon
Because it takes me back in time
When dinosaurs roamed!

Tom Beeley (9)
British International School of Stavanger, Stavanger, Norway

Norway

N orway is a beautiful country with mountains that nearly touch the clouds
O h Norway is as beautiful as a little butterfly fluttering around the flowers
R ound and round they go like a whirlwind
W andering around Norway, looking at the amazing sights
A nd non-stop fun
Y ou should try out Norway, you will see what it's like.

Hazel Highton (9)
British International School of Stavanger, Stavanger, Norway

Exploring The Wonderful World

(São Paulo)

Searching the modern city
Finding its hidden secrets,
Neon lights flashing,
Skyscrapers everywhere too!
Exploring the wonderful world!

Joshua King-Batsios
British International School of Stavanger, Stavanger, Norway

France!

F rench fries
R are sights around
A rtists and cartoonists
N othing boring
C ats wandering round
E very day waking up with fresh air and croissants.

Alisha Haroon (10)
British International School of Stavanger, Stavanger, Norway

Jungle

J ust a land of green and brown
U nder the trees so tall
N ever boring and never dead
G reat for animals to live in
L ots of resources
E veryone needs the jungle.

Nifemi Adeogba (9)
British International School of Stavanger, Stavanger, Norway

Norway

N orth, up in the north
O n the sea it is
R ushing wind
W aves crashing against the land
A nd rain pouring down
Y es, Norway it is.

Konrad Gjerstad (9)
British International School of Stavanger, Stavanger, Norway

My Bed Sheet Is Magic

Flying round the globe
On my magical flying bed sheet
Whoosh and off we go!

Oliver Lee (9)
British International School of Stavanger, Stavanger, Norway

Exploring - Haiku

The world is so vast
It is one big adventure
That's why I explore.

Daniel James Sayer (10)
British International School of Stavanger, Stavanger, Norway

The Jungle Interior

Monkeys climbing, chattering as they go,
Twigs snapping
Snakes crawling, slithering over rough ground.

Louis Arkwright (10)
British International School of Stavanger, Stavanger, Norway

Happiness

Happiness is as orange as a happy sun.
It sounds like the wind blowing.
It feels like burning water that cools down.
It tastes like melted chocolate.
It smells like a strawberry milkshake.
It looks like a bonfire, lit!
It makes me think of when I was splashing in my water pool
When it was nice and sunny.
It makes me want to go to space and see every single planet.

Marcus Hickson
Lawmuir Primary School, Bellshill

Happiness

Happiness is as pink as a rose.
It sounds like laughing and joking.
It feels like friendship.
It tastes like a chocolate milkshake.
It smells like flowers.
It looks like a daffodil.
It makes me think of my gran's chocolate muffins and
My grandad's pancakes and my mum's chocolate ice cream.
It makes me want to smile and laugh.

Hayley McCall
Lawmuir Primary School, Bellshill

Love

Love is as red as blood
It sounds like a zebra
It feels like a pillow
It tastes like a chocolate cake
It smells like flowers
It looks like muffins
It makes me think of the time Mum gave me a hug,
And when my gran kissed me.
It makes me want to smile.

Adam Brown
Lawmuir Primary School, Bellshill

Love

Love is as bright as the sun
It sounds like a baby laughing
It feels like a teddy bear
It tastes like a smoothie
It smells like a chocolate cake is cooking
It looks like the sun.

Thomas Aagesen (8)
Lawmuir Primary School, Bellshill

Happiness

Happiness as red as a rose
It sounds like our hearts
It feels like friendship has begun
It tastes like a chocolate bar
It smells like roses
It looks like flowers
It makes me think of chocolate cookies
And ice cream
It makes me want to dance.

Nickolas McInally
Lawmuir Primary School, Bellshill

Fear

Fear is as grey as a stormy night.
It sounds like the crash of two cars hitting each other.
It feels like a cactus.
It tastes like spiders' webs.
It smells like smoke and flames of life,
It looks like zombies.
It makes me think of the time when I saw a grey mouse,
It makes me feel like I want to cry.

Lauren Quinn (9)
Lawmuir Primary School, Bellshill

Happiness

Happiness is as red as a rose
It sounds like smiling
It feels like the sun
It tastes like ice cream
It smells like a bluebell
It looks like a teddy bear
It makes me think of when my little sister was born.

Josh Thompson
Lawmuir Primary School, Bellshill

Love

Love is as red as a red rose.
It sounds like a harp playing.
It feels like a bear
It tastes like a strawberry.
It smells like a sunflower.
It looks like a heart.
It makes me think of Valentine's Day.
It makes me want to smile.

Stephen Crombie
Lawmuir Primary School, Bellshill

Anger

Anger is as spooky as a haunted house
It sounds like a roaring lion
It feels like a bad dog angry
It tastes like mustard
It smells like tomato soup
It looks like the Devil
It makes me think it when my little brother gets too much attention
It makes me feel like throwing a brick out of the window.

Siobhan Donald (8)
Lawmuir Primary School, Bellshill

Anger

Anger is as red as fire.
It sounds like an explosion.
It feels like a knife.
It tastes like duck.
It smells like smoke.
It looks like the Devil.
It makes me think of Hell.
It makes me want to shout.

David Gault (8)
Lawmuir Primary School, Bellshill

Love

Love is as red as a rose,
It sounds like a beautiful butterfly,
It feels like someone giving you flowers,
It tastes like a beautiful red apple,
It smells like perfume,
It looks like someone getting married,
It makes me think of last Christmas, when I went to see Santa,
It makes me want to care for my family.

Rhianna Fowler (7)
Lawmuir Primary School, Bellshill

Happiness

Happiness is as yellow as a sun,
It sounds like laughing,
It feels like joy,
It tastes like oranges,
It smells like perfume,
It looks like a baby,
It makes me think of last year, when I went to Canada,
It makes me want to laugh.

Marc Shilliday
Lawmuir Primary School, Bellshill

Love

Love is as red as an apple,
It sounds like a violin,
It feels like a pillow,
It tastes like a chocolate milkshake,
It smells like a rose,
It looks like a little baby,
It makes me think of my family,
It makes me smile.

Ross Pender (8)
Lawmuir Primary School, Bellshill

Love

Love is as red as blood,
It sounds like a quiet voice,
It feels like somebody happy,
It tastes like strawberry milkshake,
It melts like milk,
It looks like red blood
It makes me think of when my nana Mary died a long time ago,
It makes me want to laugh and giggle.

Chloe Hogg (9)
Lawmuir Primary School, Bellshill

Love

Love is as red as a red, red rose,
It sounds like the blue sea.
It feels like a sign of friendship.
It tastes like a strawberry.
It smells like a flower.
It looks like the sunshine shining so brightly in my face.
It makes me think of when my mum gave me a big hug.
It makes me want to laugh.

Emma Marchbank
Lawmuir Primary School, Bellshill

Love

Love is as red as a rose.
It sounds like everything in the world is happy.
It feels like you are gentle in every piece of your body.
It tastes like a favourite drink.
It smells like a beautiful flower.
It looks like your happy place.
It makes me think of smiling.
It makes me want to jump about.

Kayla Cathcart
Lawmuir Primary School, Bellshill

Happiness

Happiness is as yellow as a sun
It sounds like soft waves
It feels like the sun
It tastes like a smoothie
It smells like a banana
It looks like a rose
It makes me think of the sun
It makes me want to smile.

Cameron McDougall
Lawmuir Primary School, Bellshill

Love Is

Love is as red as roses
It feels like a bear
It tastes like noodles and rice with some curry sauce.
It smells like a sunflower and blossom.
It looks like a friend.
It makes me think of a time long ago when my grandad was playing games with my family.
It makes me want to yell and shout and cry.

Amy Clemenson (8)
Lawmuir Primary School, Bellshill

Love

Love is as red as a rose,
It sounds like the wind,
It feels like a soft teddy bear,
It tastes like a piece of chocolate,
It smells like perfume,
It looks like a hot summer's day,
It makes me think of when my dad gives me a hug when I go to bed,
It makes me want to smile.

Lauren McKellar
Lawmuir Primary School, Bellshill

Sadness

Sadness is as dull as fog.
It sounds like slow waves all over the place.
It feels like a swimming pool full of tears.
It tastes like soggy cereal.
It smells like burned toast.
It looks like damp clouds.
It makes me think of when I got bullied by all of my friends, last year.

Oliver Hickson
Lawmuir Primary School, Bellshill

Love

Love is as red as a rose.
It sounds like it should be for everyone.
It feels like a favourite dinner of mine.
It tastes like apple juice form a carton.
It smells like a sweet apple.
It looks like a family always together.
It makes me think of when my mum had my little sister, Annaleas.

Chloe Clemenson
Lawmuir Primary School, Bellshill

My Mother's Desert Suitcase

(Inspired by 'The Sound Collector' by Roger McGough)

Mother went last week,
To fill her suitcase,
Full of strange noises,
From a desert far away.

Slithering of sandy lizards,
Cactuses popping up from the ground,
A whirlwind of miniature grains,
Flying like yellow birds all around.

A track from the spotted desert snake,
Hoofprints from a tired camel,
Laden with mouth watering food,
The humans were told to make.

The buzzing of mosquitoes,
The trickle of a waterfall,
A faint breeze in the leaves
Of the weary trees so tall.

Mother returned this morning,
Her case full to the brim,
Of the desert creatures, all of them in mourning
For their sounds, their minds, their friends . . .

Hannah Cicely Oliver (10)
Leighterton Primary School, Tetbury

I'm In A Golden Garden

(Inspired by 'The Sound Collector' by Roger McGough)

I'm in a golden garden,
Collecting all the sounds,
The good things only,
That I hear all around.

The twittering of the birds,
The sound of treading mankind,
The crunching of the frost,
The splashing of the wine.

The tree trunks creaking,
As they stretch in the breeze,
The leaves rustling all around me,
And all the different trees.

Butterfly wings unfolding,
As they lift off into the sky,
All the animals on the ground,
And all the animals that can fly.

Mammals, insects and beetles,
Crawling as they pass by,
Scampering squirrels and ferocious foxes,
Animals fighting, why?

Lions prowling as they commit a mighty roar,
Deer creeping forward,
Rustling the grass,
The crows give their ear-splitting caw.

I'm in a golden garden,
Closing up the box,
Hoarding all the sounds,
And clicking shut the locks.

Polly Webb (10)
Leighterton Primary School, Tetbury

My Magic Fairy Dream . . .

A treasury of fairy tales,
The pages open wide,
A carnival of joy and pain,
Adventures, trapped, inside.

Hopeful, graceful princesses,
Which Prince will soon be theirs?
Wicked, ragged sorcerers,
With gnarled green skin and hair.

Dragons, beasts and unicorns,
Alight with help and tasks,
Spoilt, wealthy rulers,
Clutching masquerading masks.

Tall castles, towers and palaces,
With turrets reaching high,
Curses flying left and right,
Up and down, but why?

For in my book, the unknown lies,
Mysteries unseen,
From time to time, I venture there,
My magic fairy dream!

Charlotte Corderoy (11)
Leighterton Primary School, Tetbury

The Mysterious Zoo

I walked around the zoo,
The zoo, I really did.

The gruesome gorilla was grooming gracefully,
By the slippery snake.

The slippery, slimy snake was strangling the chatty children.

The cheerful, chatty children were walking along by
The mad monkeys.

The mad, monstrous monkeys moaned miserably by the
Rampaging rhinoceros.

The rampaging, rough rhinoceros, was romping rapidly
By the entrance.

The entrance was by the rhinos,
The rhinos were by the monkeys,
The monkeys were by the children,
The children were by the snake,
The snake was by the gorilla,
And the gorilla was in the *zoo!*

Amy Fry (11)
Leighterton Primary School, Tetbury

A Day In The Farm Makes Noise In Itself

The quiet of the countryside
Is not quite what it seems.
The animals are off-message
And all I heard was noise:
The sound of the terrier dogs
Endless yapping into the night,
The anxious *baa* of a mother sheep
Looking for her lamb,
The deep, throaty *moo* of cows coming
In for milking,
The hiss of the cats defending
Their territory,
The satisfied, greedy *oink* of the obese pig,
The wild neigh of the bolting horse,
The stubborn *eeore* of the donkeys,
The raucous crowing of the rooster,
The homely *cluck* of the chicken.
I shut the door.
Silence at once.

Callum Sadler (11)
Leighterton Primary School, Tetbury

My Fun Frenzy Of Teachers

As the fierce Fynn goes on and on,
At a frenzy of friends fighting farts,
When joyful Jones prances around,
While the wise Wilson wails on,
And psychic Stevens sings,
And wicked Weller winks,
While truthful Trueman tells her to stop,
When cunning Kiss kicks,
While happy Harris hikes and crazy Clifford-Gaunt comments,
Yes, this jungle gym is a Jurassic level,
A golden age of fun.

Harry Palmer (10)
Leighterton Primary School, Tetbury

My Mysterious Box

(Inspired by 'Magic Box' by Kit Wright)

I found an ancient box,
With curious things inside.

The crunching of dead leaves,
Collapsing under my feet.

The twittering of fluffy, yellow chicks,
Perching in a nest.

The sound of cold, white snow,
Being flattened under my weight.

The buzzing of busy bees,
Happily collecting pollen from colourful flowers.

The sound of twigs,
Cracking under me.

The scuttling of bugs,
Running across the floor,
In my box I have all these things.

Ellie Ashley (10)
Leighterton Primary School, Tetbury

To Be Left Till Winter

All the green trees,
Dancing in the breeze.
All the floating frost,
And all of mankind's cost.
All the falling leaves,
And all the houses' keys,
And in reverse . . .
All the dead, lifeless trees,
Dancing in an imaginary breeze,
All the floating frost,
To be left till winter.

Oliver Osborne (10)
Leighterton Primary School, Tetbury

The Sound Backpack

(Inspired by 'The Sound Collector' by Roger McGough)

I strolled around the zoo
And captured all the sounds,
They clambered into my backpack,
As I looked around.

The roaring of proud lions,
The sound of crunching twigs,
The chattering of the monkeys,
Who were swinging in the trees.

The scuttling of the beetles,
The croaking from the frogs,
Bats' wings pounding the air,
As they fly around the logs.

The hissing of slithering snakes,
The gorillas beating their chests,
But by the time I get to the bush dogs,
There was no sound to be heard.

Hannah Cook (10)
Leighterton Primary School, Tetbury

The Delirious Garden

My garden is a crazy place,
A place where you should not ever venture,
Or you shall be doomed forever.

The crackling of my sister burning onions for a sacrifice,
The whooping sound of children tying up their dad,
The creaking sound of a rope with a rotten corpse,
Hung from a branch up high.

So now you see my garden is a truly crazy place,
And if you ever stroll into my garden,
Good luck to you.

Murray Thomson (11)
Leighterton Primary School, Tetbury

The Sack Of Superb Sounds

(Inspired by 'The Sound Collector' by Roger McGough)

I was walking along the street this morning
I was clutching an old sack
Carrying sounds to go on holiday
That was all I had decided to pack.

There was the sound of teachers breaking wind
My sister loudly snoring
Twigs snapping under the squirrels' dash
And the chattering trees were whispering.

The distant sound of a haunting flute
The yells of children playing
I shut my sack and silenced the sounds –
All mine.

Adam James Cox (10)
Leighterton Primary School, Tetbury

Farmyard Noises

As all the animals speak at once
The *baa* of Barry the sheep,
The *moo* of Daisy the cow.

The *crow* of Rodney the rooster
At 12pm in the evening,
The *oink* of Oliver and Miss Piggy.

The loud clatter of the stable door,
The sheer silence as the farmer Joe's footsteps
Come around the corner of the shed.

Soon as Barry, Daisy, Rodney, Oliver, Miss
Piggy and farmer Joe gathered together,
Suddenly the cat gave a massive *hisssssssss.*

Tammie Louise Scrivens (10) & Melissa Beale (11)
Leighterton Primary School, Tetbury

In The Enchanted Forest

In my box I see some things,
The sweet tinkling of fairies' wings,
As they sweep the silky leaves,
Of the enchanted forest trees.

In amongst the fields of corn,
Stands a pure gold unicorn,
Surrounded by a shimmering light,
That shines right through the starry night.

Suddenly I wake,
From my mistake,
Of falling into a dreary rest,
And dreaming of the enchanted forest.

Emanuelle Paulson (10)
Leighterton Primary School, Tetbury

There's No Kidding Me

I await at the station
With my brother P C Maison,
The train arrives, the train arrives,
We hop on, we hop on,
The station master offer me a bonbon,
I look at the bridge,
I close my eyes,
I am suddenly on the ridge,
On the ridge of the Harbour Bridge.

We pass Taronga Zoo,
I can see the monkey throwing poo at the little cockatoo,
The Opera House is as grand as a note C sharp,
I listen to the lady playing her golden harp,
The Sky Tower is as tall as Mount Everest,
Looking at it makes me feel like a tiny British guest,
There's no kidding me,
I know I'm in world-famous Sydney!

Stephanie Ruhback (10)
Malvern Parish CE Primary School, Malvern

Ghost Rides

I'm going to tell you a poem
That fits in with the day
And if you find it rubbish
Please do not say.

My favourite place is the ghost ride
That gazes into the dark
And the place that you will find them
Is in a theme park.

I hope you like it too
If you don't go on, you're a fool
I like the bit when you go in
And the ghosts are so cool.

The ghosts are not real,
They're just made out of plastic
And when you come out of the ride, you'll say
'That was fantastic!'

And you'll probably go on again
And not be scared to death
And then when you go on
Bring your cousin Beth.

Michael Brown (11)
Malvern Parish CE Primary School, Malvern

Magical Land

Mermaids swimming in the water.
In this land there is no slaughter.
Talking spiders mending ways.
Pixies talking to magic kings.
Frogs blowing bubbles in the waterfall.
The queen organising the great summer ball.
Woodland creatures having fun.
Happy times for everyone!

Bethany Wolff (9)
Malvern Parish CE Primary School, Malvern

Under The Sea

Under the sea
that's where I like to be,
with the fishes
that are not in dishes.
Swimming sharks
that are larks.
The crashing waves
uncovering caves.
Seaweed blushes
with many lushes.
Friends splashing water
not at the porter.
Lots of boats
laid out like coats.
Dripping, dancing dolphins
dancing to my song.
Graceful turtles
jumping seaweed hurdles.
I love the sea,
that's home for me!

Joanna Chappell (11)
Malvern Parish CE Primary School, Malvern

Disneyland, Florida

Wanting fame and wanting more
Mickey Mouse comes out his door!

The theme park is magical,
Absolutely dramatical.
The number of people is fanatical.
Crowds of children cheering and shouting,
Families and friends enjoying a Disney outing.

Mickey Mouse comes out his door
Wanting fame and wanting more!

Tyler Bond (11)
Malvern Parish CE Primary School, Malvern

Oscar's Old Home

Start of a journey
A piece of land worth more than money
Flowers shimmer in the wind
And the sun gives out a charming grin
A glimmer of green, brown and blue
The cattle in the next field give out a quiet *moo.*

Start of a forest, the train chugs in
To prove a rabbit and a hedgehog has seen
The trees asway
Flowers as they lay
The start of a stream
All of the leaves in the forest like pillow bursting at the seams
The train steams out of the beautiful land
Now all gone, like blown-away sand.

Brown starlight, stands out
Black wave moving about
Black eyes, never forgotten
Once last glimpse . . . cry!

Chloe Bircham (10)
Malvern Parish CE Primary School, Malvern

My Favourite Place

As fast as the train goes
You can still see the land of Pow.
When the wind blows
And the water glows,
When you swing on the tyre swing
You swing over water with your bling.

The waterfall goes to your shoulders,
But not like when you're a soldier.
I can smell apples, I can taste apples to eat.
I can see some fluffy sheep.

Olivia Rhodes (10)
Malvern Parish CE Primary School, Malvern

My Favourite Place

Come, come, come aboard this train,
As we travel the sweetness of the Swiss plains.
We travel slowly past chocolate cows, houses and fields,
Up through the mountain like a big, heavy shield.
We go faster through Kandersteg, it's a beautiful sight,
Up another mountain and back down in the night.
In the morning we go through Brig and up to Zermatt,
To see the great big Matterhorn that has lots of height.

It is time to go back, we go back the same way,
As we travel at speed I eat a Milky Way.
We pick up speed even more, I think we are breaking the law.
We whizz back through Brig but it is soon in the distance,
We travel up mountains, parachute down,
And air resistance is slowing down.
It is time to go home, we get off the train,
And suddenly I feel a spot of rain.

Lois Jones (9)
Malvern Parish CE Primary School, Malvern

I Can See My Favourite Place From My Carriage Window!

I can see my favourite place, swaying in the breeze.
I can see my favourite place, with its newly planted apple trees.
I can smell my favourite place, wafting in the wind.
I can smell my favourite place, so well I almost grinned.
I can hear my favourite place,
Laughing, whistling and that kind.
I can hear my favourite place,
Like my ears are about to unwind.
I can taste my favourite place,
The sourness almost sweet.
I can taste my favourite place . . .
But then wake up!

Emma Bradley (10)
Malvern Parish CE Primary School, Malvern

Beach

Chugging along the sandy beach,
The dark brown coconuts out of reach.
The splashing waves crashing against the rocks,
With seagulls flying in flocks.
The lorries, vans and cars driving along the road,
Carrying all the luggage, what a load!
Men and women entering the pub,
Ladies in the spa over the road, sitting on a tub.

The cliffs as high as a giant,
The pigeons flying above, causing a riot!
The sky is as blue as a fast-flowing river,
The family having a picnic of lamb liver.
The waves as high as three fully grown men,
And the flowers are about to open, but when?
The tips of the water are as white as snow,
But when will this beautiful landscape end, who knows?

Rebecca Wells (10)
Malvern Parish CE Primary School, Malvern

At The Cottage

My favourite place is the cottage,
I go there every year,
But when we finally get there,
I am awake but only near.

When I'm at the beach,
The waves lap over the tips of my toes,
And I always watch the tide,
As it comes and goes.

After I've been in the sea,
My mum gets an ice cream for me,
And when I go home, I'm never alone,
I'm safe with my family.

Andrew Pickering (10)
Malvern Parish CE Primary School, Malvern

Imagine

You use a huge key
That you plug in a tree
Through the huge tunnel we go,
Not knowing what we'll find
Yet it is full of tiny fairies
That are completely and utterly kind
You can see little pixie troupes
Flying gracefully through hoops.

Vines crawling up the tall, tall trees
And little insects such as bees
Flying around near the stream
I'm watching them as they gleam
All the smells, all the tastes, all these sights
Ogres are the only frights
All the tastes
Make me feel like I am in the right place.

Elizabeth Prior (10)
Malvern Parish CE Primary School, Malvern

Magical Land!

Skiathos, Skiathos, what a wonderful place
Skiathos, Skiathos, calm wind in my face
I've been to Skiathos so many times
So I've got enough information to fill up my rhymes
I gently lie myself down on the sand
As I drift slowly into my magical land.

After my slumber I dive in the sea
The crystal clear water covers me.
I stumble out towards a towel which I grab
Scuttling along the sand, a velvet-red crab
It nibbles intensely at my toes
And as well as us, onwards it goes.

Tobie Timmermans (11)
Malvern Parish CE Primary School, Malvern

My Magical Place!

Faster than pixies, faster than fairies,
The trees, the water and the canaries.
The trees as green as limes,
When you go past, it slows down time.
There are waterfalls and toadstools too!
And a little mouse who lives in a shoe.
I dreamt a lot when I was born
About pixies, fairies and unicorns.

The water shimmering with fairy gold,
I was destined to see this when my future was told.
And looking around I see a lily frond.
Floating around in the middle of the pond.
I've found a lot of water,
But no wall made with mortar.
I hope I'll remember this wonderful land,
And all the fairy dust I held in my hand.

Abigail Morris (9)
Malvern Parish CE Primary School, Malvern

A Magical World!

Dragons are breathing their red-hot fire,
Gnomes causing trouble at their desire.
Flying pigs gliding through the air,
Cotton-white clouds as bright as a flare.
Snow-topped mountains standing tall,
Trees on the ground, dwelling all.

Crystal ice lakes amongst the grass,
Pixies have dresses that sparkle like glass.
Food grows on trees nearby,
Snails have lessons on how to fly.
Wherever you go, you can't have less,
In this land of weirdness.

Josh Walwyn (10)
Malvern Parish CE Primary School, Malvern

My Magical Train Journey

While going past,
I'm going fast.
Through the bushes,
The fairy pushes
the goblin in the cart,
While the silver-grey dragon
Plays his part,
Going through the magical world.

The shimmering crystal river
Gives the blue gnome a shiver,
The mountain stream rushing down,
The pixie in his jewelled gown,
The poison ivy twisting round,
The ogre stepping
And making a pound,
Going through this magical world.

Anna Bradley (10)
Malvern Parish CE Primary School, Malvern

Performing A Show

People scream,
Costumes tear,
Make-up flies everywhere.
Calls ring,
Hair goes *ping,*
Until you go onstage.

Lights flash,
Cymbals clash,
Then you perform.
The audience claps,
Well done old chap,
That's how to perform a show!

Katie Reed (11)
Malvern Parish CE Primary School, Malvern

My Magical Journey

In my carriage I enter Fun Land, then I see
Pixies whizzing in the sun.
Dragons running to their nests,
Little mosquitoes being a pest.
Marram grass grows on sandy dunes,
Weird little elves, singing tunes!
The enormous daisies growing up trees,
All surrounded by swarming bees.

Tulips dancing to nursery rhymes,
Four-leaf clovers and goblins committing secret crimes.
Pebbles, shining pebbles gleaming towards the weeping willows,
With fairies sleeping on pillows.
All this from my railway carriage I see,
What a wonderful place to be!

Maddie Howell (9)
Malvern Parish CE Primary School, Malvern

Disneyland In Florida

Disneyland in Florida,
Is an amazing place,

Trying to get through the crowd,
It's horribly loud,

We finally get to Minnie and Mickey,
Although they are quite picky,

Now we're on the waterslides,
I can't wait till we get to the massive rides,

Now we have had all of the fun,
We can now enjoy the scorching sun.

Chloe Prince (11)
Malvern Parish CE Primary School, Malvern

My Favourite Place

My favourite place is France,
people eating frogs' legs
and learning how to dance.
Children playing on the beach
every day and night,
watching their dad
try and fly a kite.

Mums laughing and joking everywhere they go,
listening to Flo Rida on the radio.
That's why it's my favourite place.

Chloe Buckland (11)
Malvern Parish CE Primary School, Malvern

There's No Better Place Than My Dog's Bed

My favourite place is my doggy's bed,
even though sometimes I find it in my shed,
it may be covered in paw prints,
but the smell is raw mints.
When you go to Bouncer's bed,
it will make you relax your head,
the hair is very rare,
and anyway, it makes his bed look like a bear!

That's why my favourite place is Bouncer's bed!

Chloe Roberts
Malvern Parish CE Primary School, Malvern

I Wish I Was Away In The Ocean

I wish I was away in the ocean,
Far across the deep blue sea,
Sailing over deepest waters,
I wish I was away in the ocean,
Swimming where nobody is.
I wish it would take me far away,
I wish I was away in the ocean.

Sky Pardoe Davies (10)
Malvern Parish CE Primary School, Malvern

Italy

Italy makes you want a meal
Italy makes you go swimming while your wife is kicking someone.
Italy is a sunny place, don't worry, I'm on the case with a smiley face.
My boss is from *Italy,* he has a glittery coat.
My mum's in *Italy* with Milly, but she's hitting Billy.

Evan Wyn Jones (10)
Malvern Parish CE Primary School, Malvern

Magical Land

M onsters creeping
A boy weeping
G iants sleeping
I nsects eating
C ars beeping
A man cheating
L ost in space.

L ast man in the race
A nd a man at a pace
N ow my time is done
D one in the Magical Land.

Nathan Watts (8)
Malvern Parish CE Primary School, Malvern

Animal World!

Oh come to my animal world,
Where cheetahs and monkeys play,
They leap and climb, and
Run and race and swing in a tree all day.
Also . . .
Tigers and lions eat today,
They eat and drink,
And sleep all day.
Lambs and sheep
Bleat and *baa* all day,
Giraffe and elephant
Watch and shower,
And eat leaves from the highest tree and eat nuts.
Parrot and eagle,
They talk and squawk
And copy people and catch prey
Hyena and African dog
They laugh and eat meat
And run and fight
Oh I wish I could stay here forever.

Sarah Chappell (9)
Malvern Parish CE Primary School, Malvern

Crystal Castle

One day I walked into the woods,
I saw a crystal castle.
I could hear the sound of chatting,
I wondered who it was.
I wondered if I should go inside,
But I already had.
My dad came with me,
Then my dad saw a fairy.
She was picking some flowers,
The crystal castle was as shiny as a star.

Amy Griffiths (8)
Malvern Parish CE Primary School, Malvern

Waterfall

I walked through my garden one day,
I saw an unwanted plate.
I looked up and down,
Round and round for someone to come and take.
I started to dust the plate and I found a secret waterfall!
I heard some fairies talking,
Looking, I saw fairies flying around the bend.
The fairies saw me, screamed and flew away.
The waterfall,
The waterfall,
Splashing 'til the day is done.
There were butterflies calmly flying.
As graceful as a waterfall splashing in the sun.
Slippery stepping stones stick to the water.
The fairies had a lovely daughter.
The waterfall is a wonderful place,
So peaceful,
So calm,
The wonderful place is a lot of fun!

Aletéa Palmer-Price (8)
Malvern Parish CE Primary School, Malvern

Fairyland

As lovely as a licking leopard
As beautiful as a bumblebee
As crystal as a diamond
As tall as a waterfall
As neat as a clear swimming pool
As fun as children
As shiny as glitter
As great as gold
Have some fun and play all day
Go to sleep and have more fun the next day
So goodbye for now, see you next time, goodbye!

Naomi Chakko-George (7)
Malvern Parish CE Primary School, Malvern

Willy Wonka!

Willy Wonka's chocolate factory is a real treat.
There are lots of little people you can meet.
Its Umpa Lumpa infested,
But there's a chocolate to be tested,
'Til our big guest arrives.
We have a big chocolate river
That sometimes quivers,
But it's still a wonderful, wonderful dream.
Quick, quick, chop, chop it's 12 o'clock:
Here we are, all done,
The chocolate season has begun!

Hannah White (8)
Malvern Parish CE Primary School, Malvern

The Wizard's Tower

The magic on the tower,
Heats it up and raises up the power.
The tower is so straight,
It could be a tower of the United States.
If you go up the stairs,
You could go to secret lairs.
The tower is as tall as a hotel,
You could have a big meal.
If you want to deal,
You have to eat a big seal.

Thomas Reed (8)
Malvern Parish CE Primary School, Malvern

The Malvern Hills

As pretty as a flower,
As wet as water,
As tall as a mountain,
As green as grass,
As blue as the sky,
As yellow as the sun,
As orange as fire,
As brown as brown rocks,
As black as a monster.

Thomas Baker (7)
Malvern Parish CE Primary School, Malvern

Magical Chocolate!

C reamy!
H ot!
O rganic!
C hocolatey!
O range!
L ight!
A mazing!
T asty!
E njoy!

Adam Sturge (8)
Malvern Parish CE Primary School, Malvern

Malvern Hills

Malvern Hills, Malvern Hills as beautiful as the ocean,
Malvern Hills, Malvern Hills, as curvy as a snake,
Malvern Hills, Malvern Hills,
As beautiful as a butterfly,
Malvern Hills, Malvern Hills, as funny and sunny as a turtle
Sitting in the sun.

James Sheldrake (7)
Malvern Parish CE Primary School, Malvern

Poems

Summer is my favourite time
The sky is blue the water is fine.
In the distance I see a bumblebee buzzing in the tree.
Refreshing drinks,
Ice cream keeping cool,
Paddling in the swimming pool.
Lots of people on the sand,
Enjoying the weather across the land.

Emily Jane Standen (9)
Malvern Parish CE Primary School, Malvern

The Magical Place

In the magical place
There is a little face
Who is called the red and blue leprechaun
He was sitting on a rock eating corn
He was sitting next to a prawn eating corn
Then when the prawn was not looking
The leprechaun swallowed him whole
Then he ran, he was gone in a flash.

Jacob Chakko-George (9)
Malvern Parish CE Primary School, Malvern

My Treehouse

In my treehouse I can see a mouse
In my treehouse I can see a woodlouse
I fainted on the wooden floor
And rattled the broken door
I lay down for hours
Thinking I have powers
Then I got pulled up by a door
Now I can play with my treehouse once more.

India Timmermans (9)
Malvern Parish CE Primary School, Malvern

The Enchanted World

I was lying in bed watching the moon,
And suddenly I heard an enchanting tune.
I sat up in bed, thinking, *What's that sound*?
I opened the door, oh gosh, what I found
Was an enchanted forest.
The colours were amazing, shimmery green and everything,
It was the best thing I've ever seen.

Ellie Rose Blannin (9)
Malvern Parish CE Primary School, Malvern

The Sea

Down in the deep blue sea.
Turtle swims next to me.
Up and down and all around.
Darting fish, wild and fast.
Once I get to the bottom
I look left and right
Before the shark comes for a bite.

Thomas Prior (8)
Malvern Parish CE Primary School, Malvern

My Garden!

Don't ever sing in your garden,
Don't ever talk in your garden,
Don't ever sleep in your garden,
Don't ever leave your garden in a mess,
Don't ever do that to your garden,
For if you do, I'm pretty sure it may do something
Even worse to you.

Natasha Smith (9)
Malvern Parish CE Primary School, Malvern

Malvern Hills

As green as a frog,
As tall as a sky,
As fresh as a freezer,
As neat as a clean house,
As beautiful as a butterfly and lots and lots of trees
As fun as playing tag.

Alina Benny (8)
Malvern Parish CE Primary School, Malvern

The Sea

The sea, the sea, what a lovely place.
The turtles swimming around the rocks, swirling and whirling as they go.
Fish are playing run away, what a wonderful place to be, the sea.
Dolphins leaping, sharks are sleeping, what a marvellous place to be!

Niall Delahunty & Jake May (8)
Malvern Parish CE Primary School, Malvern

Helmms Deep

This is Hellms deep,
As cold as gold.
Armed with people with swords,
On their journey to go to a volcano.
There are going to be lots of obstacles,
Big creatures and lots of people.

James Howell (8)
Malvern Parish CE Primary School, Malvern

Summer Beach

Summer
Scalding sunshine
Lazing on the golden sand
Swimming in the shimmery sea
Swimming.

Natasha Knight (9)
Malvern Parish CE Primary School, Malvern

The Enchanted Path

The wood
Enchanted path
Bluebells, pixie houses,
Fireflies and beautiful bats.
The wood!

Georgina Smith (9)
Malvern Parish CE Primary School, Malvern

The Land Of Peace

The land of peace is a calm, calm place,
You can meet face to face.
I heard birds singing,
I saw herds of cattle and lambs,
Looking at the river dams.

Lee Woolley (7)
Malvern Parish CE Primary School, Malvern

Mythical Creatures - My Dragon

My dragon, my friend,
will follow me to the end,
he is black with red wings,
through his nose he has rings.

His name is Ferno,
he is two hundred years old,
he is very kind,
and very bold.

He lives in a cave,
at the top of a hill,
and if you go past there,
you must keep very still.

If you wake him,
a roar he will make,
and the power of the noise,
is like an earthquake.

We met on the hill,
one dark, rainy day,
he saved me from falling,
and now we are friends to play.

My dragon, my friend,
we will be always together until the end.
We have fought some battles,
and he has saved my life,
we will continue to be friends,
with courage and strife.

Matthew Hazlehurst (9)
Moorlands J&I School, West Bromwich

The Forest Tree

The awakening morning sun glistens through my branches
Bringing warmth to my heart,
Each season brings changes for my leaves,
My favourite is autumn when they turn golden brown
And flutter down to the ground,
My family surrounds me, they stay through all weathers.

The wind whispers to me in its flowing, gentle voice,
Listening to each beautiful melody of the birds,
Smelling the honeysuckle and berries' perfume,
Watching the moon rise, commanding the stars,
Fox cubs and badger, my loyal friends,
Squirrels store their winter stash within my hollow trunk.

Even though I have much happiness in my life,
I have one threat . . .

The woodcutter . . .

Rebecca Tandy (9)
Moorlands J&I School, West Bromwich

King Of The Jungle

They call me the king
With my big, great mane
I strut with pride
And roar with might.

The jungle is my kingdom
And the wide plains, my playground
I hunt with stealth
And prove my strength.

They come from far to see my glory
With fear in their eyes.
If only they knew I am as cuddly as a cat.
But then again, I don't mind being the
King of the jungle, roooaaar!

Leroy Lokko (9)
Moorlands J&I School, West Bromwich

The Mermaid

Swimming through the ocean
Swimming through the sea
Looking in the distance
Whatever could it be?

A great big shining tail
Long, flowing hair
Gracefully swimming closer
Using the ocean's flair.

This creature is smiling at me
Her hair's in a braid
This beautiful creature
Is a mermaid!

Millie Boughton (9)
Moorlands J&I School, West Bromwich

But Mom, Why Do I Have To Go To School?

Why do we have to go to school?
I know it's the law and we can't break the rule.
But why do we have to go to school?
It's not cool going to school.

'If you don't go to school, you'll end up a fool.'
'Mom, that is cruel.'

'Think of yourself as a sponge in a pool
And that the pool is your school.
You are soaking up all the water from the pool.'

Wow, I'm learning so much from being at school.
That's cool!

Emily Berry (9)
Moorlands J&I School, West Bromwich

Man With A Van

There once was a man
who had a van,
one day he got out
and ran about,
when he stopped
he had some pop,
and the lollipop man
robbed the van,
then he went home,
he started to moan,
then he said to his wife,
'I hate my life!'

Christopher Fullwood (9)
Moorlands J&I School, West Bromwich

My Mom

My mom is nice and kind
She's always on my mind
She cooks and cleans
And never is mean
Always makes me neat and clean
She never shouts or pushes me about
Only when I mess her about.

I love my mom.

Jordan Alexander (9)
Moorlands J&I School, West Bromwich

Butterfly

I went into my garden
and saw a butterfly,
its wings were very pretty
As it flew by.
It landed on a flower,
it was a sunny day,
I went to get up close
and frightened it away.

Lauren Jones (8)
Moorlands J&I School, West Bromwich

An Autumn Poem

Autumn is here, the leaves are turning gold.
The nights are getting darker and it's getting rather cold.
Some animals are getting ready to hibernate,
They are collecting food together before it's too late.
Berries ripen, fruit is ready to eat,
Winter will soon be here, when we have to turn up the heat.

Joshua Richardson (9)
Moorlands J&I School, West Bromwich

Teeth

Brush your teeth
three times a day
they will be beautiful
in half a day.
'Hip hip hooray!'
That is all I can say.

Chloe Hames (9)
Moorlands J&I School, West Bromwich

Teachers Disappearing

Teachers, teachers always say
'Don't drink water till the end of the day!'
One says they're cool, the other says, I shine'
But what Mr Michael does is just whine and whine

Double, pickle, snots and tickle
A wing of a bat
A heart of a cat
Some toes and ears
And salty tears
Double pickle, snots and tickle

Gum's forbidden
No treasure hidden
I wish they'd disappear
No tear, no fear!
How come they moan
And groan and groan?
No eating in class
I wish I'd break a glass

'Mr, can we draw?'
'No, it's against the law!'

'Mr, can we dance?'
'Not another chance!'

'We want freedom!
We want to play!'
But all they say is, '*Go away!'*

Double, pickle, snots and tickle
A heart of a pig
A rotten twig
A nail
A snail

Teachers! Leave us alone!
I sure will miss Mr Michael's groan!

Shahed Ali Al-Nadabi (11)
Muscat International School, Ruwi, Sultanate of Oman

Teacher Disappearing

She doesn't let me open my face book
So, I wish I could tear up her mark book!
Or, hang her on a tree with a hook.
Sometimes she says we are stupid
And she loves Cupid!

Some hair from a boy's armpit,
And a little annoying kid,
Girl's lovely bangs and skin that is tanned
Boys that failed to send a mail,
Are all under my spell,
Pop it all in my cauldron,
Before I say, 'Make my teacher disappear!'

I would like to learn about an unknown man called Poe,
Instead of Alexet Zoë,
The teacher tells me not to wear any scarf,
When one day I saw her wearing one which made me laugh,
She says MIS is not 'Bellwood'
So I will make sure it is 'Hollywood'.

Blood from whale,
Seven thousand-feet snail,
Three thousand calories of fat,
And I would not forget bats and rats,
Elephants' poo, saliva too,
Spider's eye and snake's heart.
Pop it into my cauldron before I say, 'Make my teacher disappear!'

She doesn't have four eyes but six eyes,
She smells when she passes by.
She needs to have plastic surgery,
I would prefer if she taught music in a nursery.

Girl's blonde hair, boy's armpit hair,
Take them before they tear,
Toilet water from the gutter,
Little bit of frog's leg,
Some old rotten, egg,
Rotten snake,

Bee's milkshake,
Let it bake,
Put it all into my cauldron
Before I say, 'Make my teacher disappear!'
If they don't I will pull their ear!

Fatima Hussain (11)
Muscat International School, Ruwi, Sultanate of Oman

Teachers Disappearing

Teachers, teachers, are so hyper
I think that they're weird and sometimes stink like a diaper.
When I see them running, I think that they're kind of a fool
But when I see them kidding us, I think that they rule the school
Some of them look like a bunny
And some of them are major funny
So I want all the teachers to go away
But if they come back I would like to hear them say,
'You have a holiday for the rest of the day.'
I'm going to make a spell so that they can go away
And I wish it to work so I'm going to say
The spell that I did it on my way.

An eye from a dead fly
A poison spider so that they can die
A skunk's stinky fart
A brain and a heart
From a human's body part

A little piece of a monkey's hair
A huge, sparkling, black chair
A donkey's tail
And a big blue whale
A dog's pink tongue
And a human's lung.

Students, students have no fear
Because all the teachers will definitely disappear.

Khadija Fardan Al-Hamdany (12)
Muscat International School, Ruwi, Sultanate of Oman

Teachers Disappearing

In the world where children are to be free,
There come teachers, leading us to be people in ironed clothes,
Smiling bright.
Looking in the mirror gives us a fright.
If you go against their law
They go steamy and red in the face.
Oh! Teachers are a weird and scary case.

We finally, for our problem, find a solution
It is to make a vanishing potion
The ingredients are hard to find
But we do want to get rid of the teachers
And secure our minds

Hickory, Dickory, boil and burn the lotion
Make this charm help our potion.

Zebra's tail and spider's legs
Bear's fur and bee's eggs
A snake's tongue and its head
A bat's eye and pencil lead
A shoelace and a smelly sock
A bicycle and a rusted chain lock
Throw them in a cauldron full of snot
Throw in some rotten garlic when the stove is hot.

Hickory, Dickory, boil and burn the lotion
Make this charm help our potion.

After a while we stir the cauldron with a spoon
We keep on going clockwise till it's noon
Then we throw in the hairs of the teachers we want to vanish
Then, when it's all over, we are free to enjoy a day
at the sea, Cornish

Hickory, Dickory, boil and burn the lotion
Make this charm help our potion.

A few ingredients left for our dreams to come true
And the teachers who are about to vanish have no clue
Some baboon's blood and Dracula's nails
Rhinos' horns and rabbits' tails

Washing powder and powder puff
Thirty four erasers and that's enough

Hickory, Dickory, boil and burn the lotion
Make this charm help our potion.

Amna Aftab (11)
Muscat International School, Ruwi, Sultanate of Oman

The Magical Paper (Origami)

With practised hands
And careful skill,
You can create
Existence at will,

It is an art
That has suffered neglect,
Teach it to others
And have an effect,

Know the power
Of the folding,
The very same skill
You are holding,

Everyone has it,
It comes from inside,
So let it all out,
There's nothing to hide,

Only the ones
That disbelieve,
Discard the talent
That cannot conceive,

Heed my advice
And my warnings as well,
Now it's time
To bid you farewell.

Yousef Al Riyami (10)
Muscat International School, Ruwi, Sultanate of Oman

Teachers Disappearing

Teachers, teachers, the way you treat us
Continuously making me shave my hair!

Teachers sometimes treat us nice
Surviving class is like rolling a dice
If I wear eyeliner, I'll grab their attention,
I'll have to remove it or else I'll get detention

Teachers, teachers, the way you treat us
Continuously making me shave my hair!

Dead lizard and monkey's tail
Vomit of a man that was in jail
Blood of a bear, heart of a snail
Human's wing and a pig's tail.

Teachers, teachers, the way you treat us
Continuously making me shave my hair!

With hair of a wolf and bird's wing
Cat's mouth, the spell I'll sing
Rabbit's vomit, frog's eyes
A donkey's foot and a piece of ice

Teachers, teachers, the way you treat us
Continuously making me shave my hair!

Durk's braces, man's spit
Lion's nails, we'll make them fit
Rabbit's saliva and nose of a fox
Bones of an elephant and a spider box

Teachers, teachers, the way you treat us
Continuously making me shave my hair!

Now my evil spell is over
And my pot I'll cover
You'll disappear, there'll be no proof

One, two, three *poof!*

Nicole Vacca (11)
Muscat International School, Ruwi, Sultanate of Oman

Teachers Disappearing

Teachers, teachers, stop following me everywhere!
I can't even concentrate on my messy hair!

Teachers are weird creatures
Because they have horrible features,
They give us useless homework,
I wish some day I could eat them with a fork!

Teachers, teachers, stop following me everywhere!
I can't even concentrate on my messy hair!

An eye from a poisonous toad,
A tail of a rat found on the road,
A donkey's yellow tooth,
And a hamster's fur which has to be smooth.

Teachers, teachers, stop following me everywhere!
I can't even concentrate on my messy hair!

A poisonous sting from a bumblebee,
A dead leaf from an oak tree,
A web from a spider,
A foot of a horse and the shoe of his rider.

Teachers, teachers, stop following me everywhere!
I can't even concentrate on my messy hair!

Liver from a goat,
And a dead fish on a boat,
Lion's claws,
And milk from an ugly cow.

Teachers, teachers, stop following me everywhere!
I can't even concentrate on my messy hair!

Cool it with a hair from Orlando Bloom
Give it to a teacher, and a spell should go

Boom!

Sherine Bou Dargham (11)
Muscat International School, Ruwi, Sultanate of Oman

Teachers Disappearing

Teachers, always whining
When they are happy they are shining
When they are angry they give detention
Because you don't pay attention

Scale of snake, heart of dragon
Blood of wolf
Teachers, teachers, turn to rubble
I want to play bubble trouble

Teachers always run
Because they are running from the sun
Evil, evil everywhere
Students run away when teachers stare
When teachers look at you, you can't
Because of their ear hairs

Human corpse, teacher's blood
Coldstone and hot dragon stud
Tickle, tickle, pig's pickle
Always act like a popsicle

Teachers, teachers, always mad
And in class you can't say, 'Lad'
Wrinkles, wrinkles everywhere
Teachers, teachers beware

Human shoe, eye of newt, a piece of hair
And tree root, pure water, toad tongue
Teachers, teachers, turn to rum

Teachers, teachers always mad
If a student is sad
All teachers everywhere
Get in the cauldron
And disappear.

Seif Alhajri (12)
Muscat International School, Ruwi, Sultanate of Oman

Teachers Disappearing

Teachers, teachers, always whining
They think they are very shining
Silly, silly, why are you silly?
They ask us to be thrilly

Double, double, toil and trouble
Fire burn and cauldron bubble

A dead fly's wing
And a gypsy's ring
An owl's eye
And teacher's stinking tie

Double, double, toil and trouble
Fire burn and cauldron bubble

They think they are very smart
But they smell like fart
Their legs are skinny
They think we are mini

Double, double, toil and trouble
Fire burn and cauldron bubble

They think our brains are dirt
They tell us to wear a neat, clean shirt
Add some fungus pickle
And then try to tickle

Double, double, toil and trouble
Fire burn and cauldron bubble

You will have a perfect potion
To make the boring teachers disappear.
Try it!

Sana Shahid (11)
Muscat International School, Ruwi, Sultanate of Oman

Teachers Disappearing

Teachers make you fear
Everything till you shed a tear
Staring at you trying to find something to get you in trouble
Be careful if you're chewing, don't blow a bubble!

Gather some used gum
Lower the lights and bang the drum
Cut their mouth
Then kick them south

Da double, dee double dee
Make teachers disappear then I'll be forever free

Grab their spit
And some hair from their pit
One of Mr Michael's toes
And if you can, bring along his nose

Da double, dee double dee
Make teachers disappear then I'll be forever free

Add the finger of a monkey
And the tail of a donkey
The eye of a snake
Cool it with a snowflake

Da double, dee double dee
Make teachers disappear then I'll be forever free

Close your eyes
Then tell no lies
Wait until you see purple mice
Then look out the window, you'll see a teacher that flies.

Wasan Al Bulushi (11)
Muscat International School, Ruwi, Sultanate of Oman

Teachers Disappearing

Teachers, teachers, always boring
Teachers, teachers, always annoying
'Sit! Write! Shut up and read!' they say.

'Sit up straight, don't pick your nose
You're my slave, you have to obey.'

Cook up a recipe to make them go away
Fantastic idea, no more teachers to obey!

A lizard's tongue, some bear poo
Troll's spit, cow's snot, put that in too
Boy's sweat, girl's hair
Hang on, sit, watch and stare
We'll turn the teachers into creatures.

Armpit hair, cat earwax
Chop off some toad heads with an axe
The stomach of a rat
Tooth of a vampire and eye of bat
Look for earthworms in the soil
Oh, we'll steam the teachers in boiling oil.

Fizz! Sizzle! Boom! Splat! The teachers disappear
We hope they never reappear
All the children prancing
Girls lift up their skirts and start singing and dancing
No more teachers to obey!
What a joyful, pleasant day!
Hooray!
Hooray!

Lujainah Talal Saif Al-Subhi (11)
Muscat International School, Ruwi, Sultanate of Oman

Teachers Disappearing

Teachers, teachers, always mad,
Teachers, teachers, please be glad.
I want to eat gum every day,
But they always say, *'No way, no way!'*

Flap like a bird, jump like a fish
Sit down, stand up, wish, wish, wish
The puke of a cat
A wing of a bat

A baboon's spit
The teacher's pit
A goat's skin
A vampire's chin

Flap like a bird, jump like a fish
Sit down, stand up, wish, wish, wish
A heart of a pig
A leg on a stick

An eye of an owl
Some petals from a flower
A hyena's toes
A dead human's nose

Now the teacher's disappeared
Yeah, yeah!
Now the teacher's disappeared
Hooray! Hooray!

Iram Al-Ghafri (12)
Muscat International School, Ruwi, Sultanate of Oman

Pets

P ets are good
E agles' friends
T rusting people
S ociable to other pets.

Azim Baruno (9)
Muscat International School, Ruwi, Sultanate of Oman

Teachers Disappearing

Teachers, teachers, why are you yelling?
Oh my gosh, my brain is shaking,
Always filling our brain with rubbish
And if you go away that's what I wish!

Some bits of worms and some germs
Would help out with the school terms
Bubblegum would stick their butts to the chair
And won't let them care.

Teaches, teachers, why are you yelling?
Oh my gosh, my brain is shaking,
Give me a slimy squiggler from the sea,
And a poisonous sting of a bumblebee.

Will the teacher explode
Or will the teacher go flying down the road?
Who knows?
Not I, let's wait and see!

Teachers, teachers, why are you yelling?
Oh my gosh my brain is shaking,
The juice from the fruit of the ju-jube tree,
And the powdered bone of a wombat's knee.

I'll stir them all up and boil them long,
A mixture tough, a mixture strong,
And one hundred other things as well,
Each with a rather nasty smell.

Katya Plotnikova (11)
Muscat International School, Ruwi, Sultanate of Oman

Teacher Disappearing

Double, double, blood and trouble,
Fire burns that makes a bubble.
Teachers always give detentions,
And even worse, suspensions,
Always angry, mad and serious,
I want to cook him and make him delicious.

Double, double, blood and trouble,
Fire burns that makes a bubble.
Scale of fish, tooth of tiger,
A red mouth of a liar,
Tooth of wolf, tails from mice,
That makes it really, really nice.

Double, double, blood and trouble,
Fire burns that makes a bubble.
A baboon butt that has a bite,
Chicken wings that fly like a kite,
A brown ear, tongue from a frog,
Can you please give me a log?

Double, double, blood and trouble,
Fire burns that makes a bubble.
As sweet as a candy, sour like vinegar,
The potion is hot and orange like a tiger,
Cool it with a baboon's blood,
Then the charm is firm and good.

Muhammad Naufal (12)
Muscat International School, Ruwi, Sultanate of Oman

Teacher Disappearing

Teacher, teacher, always whining
Teacher is always shining
Teacher is boring
Because he is always snoring

Double, double, toil and trouble,
Fire burn and cauldron bubble

Poisoned water with snail's eyes
Eagle wings and shoe ties
I put in some hair that was cool
I mixed it with a slimy pool

Double, double, toil and trouble,
Fire burn and cauldron bubble

I put in all my ingredients
I will start my spell
He has too much spell
Someone rang the bell

Double, double, toil and trouble,
Fire burn and cauldron bubble

Mix the ingredients all together
They will turn into a feather

Double, double, toil and trouble,
Fire burn and cauldron bubble.

Syed Hassan Imam (12)
Muscat International School, Ruwi, Sultanate of Oman

Teachers Disappearing

Teachers, teachers, always whine and whine
When they get really mad they hit us with a vine
Teachers, teachers never care, only when they've been dared

Bubble, trouble, boiling bubble
Stop making me get in trouble

Leg of a dog
And a bunch of logs
A slice of cheese
And a group of fleas

Bubble, trouble, boiling bubble
Stop making me get in trouble

Ears of monkey
A heart of a donkey
Skin of a lizard
A hat of a wizard

Bubble, trouble, boiling bubble
Stop making me get in trouble

A teacher's legs
And dragon eggs
A slimy head
And brown bread.

Now the potion is ready to be used.

Ruwaid Al Habbi (13)
Muscat International School, Ruwi, Sultanate of Oman

Teachers Disappearing

Teachers, teachers, very mean.
The meanest people I've ever seen.
Homework and homework every day.
They've done too much, now they'll have to pay.

Double, double, toil and trouble
Fire burn and cauldron bubble.

Toad legs, werewolves' nails,
Serpent tongue and dragon tails.
Cockroach hands, trunk of an elephant.
Bones of a fish and the heart of an ant.

Double, double, toil and trouble
Fire burn and cauldron bubble.

Frog eyes, the mane of a horse.
Scorpion blood and a spell of course.
Cast the spell to make a liquid.
The potion looks like poisonous fluid.

Double, double, toil and trouble
Fire burn and cauldron bubble.

Teachers, teachers, all disappear
So that we don't have any fear
Of all the homework you will give
And that we can peacefully live.

Rifat Hassan (11)
Muscat International School, Ruwi, Sultanate of Oman

Teachers Disappearing

Teachers, teachers, always whining,
Stupid teachers think they're shining,
Always talking in your ear,
Make the teachers disappear.

Double, double, toil and trouble,
Fire burn and cauldron bubble.

Adder's fork, blind worm's sting,
A brand new phone, a bloodstained ring,
A lizard's leg, a human eye,
A stinking teacher's clip-on tie.

Double, double, toil and trouble,
Fire burn and cauldron bubble.

Brain of fish, lock of hair,
Throw in Mr Michael without a care,
Monkey tail, wing of bat,
Greyhound's ear, tooth of rat.

Double, double, toil and trouble,
Fire burn and cauldron bubble.

Teachers, teachers, always whining,
Stupid teachers think they're shining,
Always talking in your ear,
Make the teachers disappear!

Casey Beatson (12)
Muscat International School, Ruwi, Sultanate of Oman

Teachers Disappearing

Teachers, teachers, always whining
Dumb teachers think they are shining
They twist your ear
They pull your hair

Double, double, toil and trouble
Fire burn and cauldron bubble

A monkey's heart, a shark's fart
A skunk's tail and a donkey's nail
Let's mix them together and tell
The teachers' disappearing spell

Double, double, toil and trouble
Fire burn and cauldron bubble

Teacher, oh teacher, I wish you wouldn't be
Teacher, oh teacher, I wish you would disappear
Teacher, oh teacher, I feel like covering you in ink
Teacher, oh teacher, you stink

Double, double, toil and trouble
Fire burn and cauldron bubble

After mixing the baboon's head
And lizards which were dead
Then the teachers were fed
And then in a second the teachers had disappeared or were dead.

Aimen Haider (11)
Muscat International School, Ruwi, Sultanate of Oman

Teachers Disappearing

Teachers, teachers, always whining,
When the students are shining.
They give you detention,
There is even worse, suspension!

Double, double, toil and trouble
Fire, fire, boil the mixture and make some bubbles

Brain of a baboon, picture of a cartoon
Eyes of a newt, a toe from a smelly foot
Scale of a crocodile, a ripped teacher's file
Chapatti from Ruwaid and a six of spades

Double, double, toil and trouble
Fire, fire, boil the mixture and make some bubbles

Tongue of a rat, teeth of a bat
Feather of a bird, glasses from a nerd
Skin of a snake, some fish from the lake
A butterfly's cocoon and a piece of the moon

Double, double, toil and trouble
Fire, fire, boil the mixture and make some bubbles

Teachers, teachers go away
Never come back any day.
Teachers, teachers, disappear
So we can be happier.

Assam Munir (12)
Muscat International School, Ruwi, Sultanate of Oman

Teachers Disappearing

Blue, white and black
No scarves or hats!
Tuck in your shirt, tie up your hair
Only blue, white and black underwear

Bubble, gouble, double, triple the trouble
All in my big black cauldron

Cooked cats' poop
With a lot of broccoli soup
A dozen disgusting lizard scales
For all teachers who make us fail

Bubble, gouble, double, triple the trouble
All in my big black cauldron

A dozen rotten werewolves' toes
And an enormous amount of mummies' heads, gross
Fish and all sea creatures
For all Ish, maths, French and music teachers.

Bubble, gouble, triple the trouble
All in my big black cauldron

Five chopped intestines of mice
And ten humungous jars of lice
Make all the teachers with all of their features
Disappear.

Haneen Ahmad Rashed Ibrahim (11)
Muscat International School, Ruwi, Sultanate of Oman

Teachers Disappearing

Teachers, teachers, you give us books to break our backs
You give us homework, stack by stack
Teachers give detentions, that's child cruelty, they should go to jail
They laugh in your face when you fail

Double, double, toil and trouble
Fire burn and cauldron bubble

In the pot goes a pig's eye
A baby bird that cannot fly
A cobra's venom and a dragon's tail
A studded, broken tiger nail

Double, double, toil and trouble
Fire burn and cauldron bubble

A rat's tooth and a dog's lung
A crab's claw and whale's tongue
A scorpion's sting
And a broken eagle's wing

Double, double, toil and trouble
Fire burn and cauldron bubble

Teachers, please go away
If you will you'll make my day
Double, double, toil and trouble
Fire burn and cauldron bubble.

Yousuf Al-Mahrooqi (7)
Muscat International School, Ruwi, Sultanate of Oman

Penguins

Penguins are noisy and they're white and black,
they have a long nose and their legs are so small
and they slide everywhere.
They live in Antarctica.
The egg is weird and the mother goes to hunt fish,
but some of the mothers die because sharks eat them.

Tamima Al Shanfari (9)
Muscat International School, Ruwi, Sultanate of Oman

Pirates

Captain Peter
Is tough and strong,
All day sneaking around.
He leaves the ship
And goes eating,
But all they say is,
'Yeah, Captain Peter.'
They think he is kind of mean
Or just nasty,
But he hates his crew,
John and Blasty.
They forgive him and
Give him lollies and candy.
Why don't they understand
That he lost his leg?
And don't you see,
He can't even lean?
Can't you see he is mean
And cranky?
He also lost his special hanky.
Now let's end this poem of Captain Peter,
Maybe he will return and wake up
And eat you up.

Malak Al Nadabi (9)
Muscat International School, Ruwi, Sultanate of Oman

Family

F ather cares about me
A nd I love him very much
M other loves me all the time
I also love her very much
L ove never ends in a happy family
Y ou will want a happy family like that, won't you?
Well, this is my happy family.

Xiao Wensherg Xiao (9)
Muscat International School, Ruwi, Sultanate of Oman

Teachers Disappearing

Teachers, teachers, always annoying
Teachers, teachers, always snoring

They always tick
They always stink

Double, double, make some bubble
Please go away
Never come back anyway

Ring the bell, make some spell
A dinosaur's eyeball
And a ripped off basketball
A heart of a dead dog
And an eye of a short frog

A finger of a girl
And a tank of a squirrel
Blood slime
Vinegar and lime
Thrice and once add a hairy spider
Thrice and twice add the eye of a tiger
A donkey tail with a stinky blue whale
Human arm for a charm
Now your spell is ready, so get ready!

Tegan Al-Harthi (11)
Muscat International School, Ruwi, Sultanate of Oman

Animals

Ants live in a colony, for sugar they die.
Naga in Malay means dragons, they like to fry.
Iguanas are disgusting, about this I do not lie.
Monkeys make a lot of noise, I do not know why.
Antelopes jump and run, they say 'Bye-bye!'
Llamas live in South America on a land that is dry.
Sharks can swim, but they can't fly.

Fauzan Nor Azmi (9)
Muscat International School, Ruwi, Sultanate of Oman

Teachers Disappearing

Teachers, teachers, always scream
    And taste like sour cream
Teachers, teachers are always late
I guess they're on their first date
Teacher, teachers always cry
    They are wet and dry

Bridle, bridle on the freckle
    Tiny fingers tickle, tickle

A parrot's beak
Filled with lots of geeks
A nerd's brain
For the fire to gain
A stinky sock
A smelly fox
Cockroach skin
Eagles' fins
A dog's stinky
Smelly nails
A lizard's tail

Bridle, bridle on the freckle
    Tiny fingers tickle, tickle.

Swafiya Sheikh (11)
Muscat International School, Ruwi, Sultanate of Oman

Animals

A nimals are cute
N ever kill them because they're nice
I love animals, I hope you do too
M y whole family loves animals
A nd cares about them more
L ives we save, you feel like a hero
S hare love with animals.

Jasmine Craven (9)
Muscat International School, Ruwi, Sultanate of Oman

Teachers Be Gone

Oh teachers, they always complain
They don't know how much happiness they drain.
'Do this, do that'
It makes you want to fall flat.

Now the spell
For which many have fell!
An otter's chest
An old man's vest

A lion's rumble
Makes teachers tumble

Put in three bloodstained textbooks
And seventeen crooked fish hooks
A severed toe
The wings of a crow

A lion's rumble
Makes teachers tumble.

An elephant's hair
The eye of a bear
Now put on a lid
And the spell is solid.

Maha Al-Balushi (11)
Muscat International School, Ruwi, Sultanate of Oman

Penguin

P enguins are fat.
E nding with baby wearing a hat.
N ow it is cold.
G oing to Antarctica.
U sed to cold and not hot.
I n their hearts they love everyone.
N ow you know, please let me go!

Reem Ali (9)
Muscat International School, Ruwi, Sultanate of Oman

My Dog

My dog does
Two things
In the morning
Scratch, stretch
My dog does
Three things
In the afternoon
Play, sleep, run
My dog does
Four things
In the evening,
Have
Fun, mess up
Bathing and walking
My dog does
Five things
At night
Like . . .
Eat, drink
Get a smelly perfume salon treatment and sit
In the middle of the night, my dog sleeps.

Maha Raya (8)
Muscat International School, Ruwi, Sultanate of Oman

Teachers Disappearing

Teachers, teaches, always swearing
And never sharing

Always on a date then we get a break
Once they're dumped, we're left with junk

They think they're cool but let's show the fools
Who actually rule in that school.

Mix, mix, make them into our slaves!

We're punks and like to funk
So put in a frog's lung
Because they're full of junk in their trunk
We always do a lot of mess
So put less homework and more fun
Cos when we're gone, we leave them with stress.

A pinch of cockroach poo
And get Mr Michael's traffic lights
And mix them all around.

Mix, mix, make them into our slaves!

Amira Al Jabri (11)
Muscat International School, Ruwi, Sultanate of Oman

Teachers Disappearing

Double, double, toilet trouble
This teacher is always muddled
She will never get hit by the arrows of Cupid
She is always mean and stupid

Double, double, toilet trouble
Put some lizard scale
Put some monkey spit
Add a disgusting snail

Double, double, toilet trouble
Throw in five teacher heads
Add some elephant fart
Then tear a teacher to shreds
Then put in a glass of dinosaur pee
Teachers, teachers, think they're cool

Teachers, teachers, think they're cool
But I think they're just fools
Add one touch of her poo
And stir the cauldron.

Mudrick Mussa (12)
Muscat International School, Ruwi, Sultanate of Oman

Teachers Disappearing

Teachers, teachers, always whining
They just want us always shining
They are unbelievably boring
And we are sleeping and snoring

To make a teacher disappear
We need a frog's stomach and heart
That will take us to the start
Double, trouble, let's make some bubbles

Add some poison from a snake
Take some dead fish from a lake
That was as simple as a piece of cake
Double, trouble, let's make trouble

Now the teacher's disappeared
Finally no pinching and shouting in the ear
Now they're smear, now no fear
Bye-bye teacher
Now no treating us like creatures.

Elay Nasser Mubarak Al-Araimi (10)
Muscat International School, Ruwi, Sultanate of Oman

Teachers Disappearing

Teachers, teachers, always whining.
Teachers stay always shining.
Teachers could be stupid if you don't do the homework.
They are the teachers of Cupid.

Blood of a tiger, a liver of a leopard.
Blood of a baboon, a toe of an ostrich.
Web of a spider, hair of a sheep.
A poop of a turtle, blood of a jaguar.

Double, double, tails and toes.
Double, double, they make us grouse.
Double, double, they get angry.
Double, double, meat of rat with sauce of poop.

Teachers, teachers, every time funny.
Teachers, teachers, every time cool.
Teachers, teachers, let us learn.
Teachers, teachers, every time talking.

Azzam Abdullah Ali Al-Nabri (12)
Muscat International School, Ruwi, Sultanate of Oman

Teachers Disappearing

Double, double, toilet trouble
These teachers are crazy and stupid
But they aren't even close to Cupid
Always coming to class late
But I think they went on a date

Double, double, toilet trouble
Take a monkey and throw like an ocean
Add a lizard leg in your potion

Double, double, toilet trouble
Teachers think that they are smart
But I think they are stupid, like Bart
Asking me, they aren't smart
But the class smells because they fart

Double, double, toilet trouble
They are just boring like nerds
But they think they are cute like a bird.

Sarosh Shahid Al-Querish (12)
Muscat International School, Ruwi, Sultanate of Oman

Teachers Disappearing

Teachers, teachers, always eating
Eating bubblegum and killing
In Arabic I am asleep
Sleeping, sleeping so deep

Double, double, toil and trouble
Fire burn and cauldron bubble
Farting Cyclops and vampire blood
Lizard's head and a bit of lion in a flood

A sprinkle of poop
And some soup
Snake's poison and Cyclop's eye
Lion's tail and girl's hair dye

Teachers, teachers, see you later
I will leave you now in a vapour
Try not disappearing, the fire will kill
And I will have fun laughing at you peeing your pants.

Mohammed Hussain Al-Nabhani
Muscat International School, Ruwi, Sultanate of Oman

Teachers Disappearing

Teachers, creatures, always screaming
So angry their faces are steaming
Not so bothered to come to school
Teachers always make us look uncool

A bit of snot, blood of fish
Rotten flowers, a little child's kiss
An octopus's tentacle, a spider's eye
A teacher's ear, and say bye-bye

Juice of mint, a pinch of salt
Candies and chocolate malt
False teeth straight from a grandma
Gruesome things like blood from a llama

What do you think of my spell?
Just go ahead and tell . . .
Now the teachers are disappearing
One by one and that's what I'm seeing.

Ramsha Khalid (11)
Muscat International School, Ruwi, Sultanate of Oman

No More Bossy Teachers

All the teachers always complaining
Teachers, they are always explaining
They make school look boring
And at night they can't stop snoring

One litre of vomit and a liver from a dog
A broken skull and a jar of a mystery fog
A burned bag with some burned books
A sheet with a failed test and some sharp hooks

A broken clock with a weird *tick-tock*
An eye from a stupid hawk
Snake scale and an alligator's tail
And a fish that is ready to bail

All the teachers always complaining
Teachers, they are always explaining
Now we will make them pay,
This spell will make them go away!

Mohammed Abdullah Khalid (12)
Muscat International School, Ruwi, Sultanate of Oman

Teachers Evaporate

Teachers, teachers, always whining
They are always shining
They never let us eat bubble
They are the biggest trouble

Ask someone an easy way
Try to find a tricky way
We are happy, trouble away
If trouble away

They always talk like a rat
They are much too fat
They make us fear
Never go near

Teachers, teachers, always lining
Sometimes like teeth grinding
But I love it when their faces are smiling.

Hind (11)
Muscat International School, Ruwi, Sultanate of Oman

Teachers Disappearing

Teachers, teachers, always so boring, I will end up snoring

So cruel, especially at school
Bring out the cauldron for all these fools
So we can get out of our schools
They always say, 'Tuck in your shirt,' 'Look at your skirt.'

Teachers, teachers, disgusting creatures

Put in a dragon's fart and a frog's heart
And never forget a wrinkled shirt and a ripped skirt
A turtle's shell to cast this spell
Don't forget some gum to show we're not dumb
A witch's ear wax because they don't pay their tax

Teachers, teachers, full of junk, they never like funk!

Najla (11)
Muscat International School, Ruwi, Sultanate of Oman

Teachers Disappearing

Teachers, teachers are so boring
Some day I will end up snoring

They shout, they scream, they never nag for ice cream,
They're smart but still stupid.

Pink hair, dog's saliva, Zainah's curly hair
And Tamather's silky hair.

Teachers, teachers are so boring
Some day I will end up snoring
Teachers, teachers are such aggressive creatures.

Pink hair, dog's saliva, my brother's snot
And some hairy moles and nerd's brain.

Teachers, teachers are so boring
Some day I will end up snoring
Teachers, teachers are so amateurish.

Manal Al Azri (12)
Muscat International School, Ruwi, Sultanate of Oman

Teachers Disappearing

Teachers, teachers - bossy, pathetic, tall and short
Teachers, teachers - whining, never smiling, all that sort

Homework, homework has to be done every day
If we don't they say, 'You have to obey.'

Teachers, teachers, stinky creatures
Holding a stick for all kinds of cheaters
Common witches let them disappear with half the body of a deer
A dog's puke
A dragon's mouldy nail
And a skunk's tail, a lion's eye and for some ants we say goodbye.
My sister's bow, my uncle's saw, my brother's toe and here they go!

Gim, gim, paka, paka, pah, lam, lam, bam, dam
Common trouble, make some bubble and make it double.
No more teachers, no more ugly features.

Zainah Hassan (11)
Muscat International School, Ruwi, Sultanate of Oman

Teachers Disappearing

Teachers, teachers, always whining
When the sun is shining
They look stupid
And they are meaner than Cupid.

Round about the cauldron go;
In the dead man's brain and heart
Frogs' poop and logs' ash
Blind eyes and mutated flies.

In the plant fertiliser and sewer water
Dead pigs and rotten tomatoes
Mummy's snot and a dead fish

Teachers, teachers, disappear
And never reappear
Leave us in freedom and joy.

Mohammed Al-Wahaibi (11)
Muscat International School, Ruwi, Sultanate of Oman

Teachers Disappearing

Teachers, teachers, always screaming
When something falls they're always leaning
They look crazy
And sometimes lazy.

Round about the cauldron go;
Dead man's kidney, in we throw
Frogs' entrails and a lot of coloured dyes
Plant fertiliser and legendary lies.

The dead cow's heart, in we throw
Frog poop and rotten, dead mouse
A human's head and a fifty-year-old house
Chicken's hair and blind eyes

Teachers, teachers, you will disappear
And please never reappear.

Taimur Fatik Fahar Alsaid (11)
Muscat International School, Ruwi, Sultanate of Oman

Lapland In Winter

Lapland is special
As valuable as gold
Hot chocolate is the winter drink
It's easy to ski
A couple of lessons
Got it straightaway
Some hills are steep, some are not.
They speak Finnish, some speak English
Skiing is real
The sweets were wonderful
Better than chocolate
On the last day everything seemed to go
But the good thing was
I made some friends
All in the week.

Lewis Birch (9)
Rufford CE Primary School, Ormskirk

The Runaway Spring

There was a boy, Jake
and he had a little spring
until he knocked it off the table
and it bounced and went *ping!*

Bounce around the classroom
bounce around the school
bounce around the playground
Then someone said, 'Cool!'

Bouncing, running everywhere
round the place
scrambling, brawling here and there
all around the place

Everyone's running around the school
topsy-turvy, turvy-topsy
everyone's dashing round the school
tripping up, being bopsy

Then the spring bounced into the classroom
and onto the table
'Phew,' said everybody
'Where have you all been?' said Mrs Mable
'It's time for lessons!'

Jim Quinlan (9)
Rufford CE Primary School, Ormskirk

The River Of Life

Life is like a river
Sometimes rocky, sometimes smooth
Life is sometimes fast and other times slow
We have hard times like ice
And nice times like summer
We wish it would go on forever
But alas, like a river, it has to end.

Amelia Hickson (10)
Rufford CE Primary School, Ormskirk

Zoom!

Forget Ferrari
Forget Porsche
There's a new car on the block
It's called?
Rock?
Block?
Wow, that's fast!

It's slick and gold
It stands out very bold
Leather seats
It beats the rest
Wow, that's fast!

I wonder what the name is
Whoosh?
Push?
Rush?
Slush?
I know, *Zoom!*
Wow, that's fast!

Jakob Blundell (9)
Rufford CE Primary School, Ormskirk

Lionel Messi

Lionel Messi is the best,
Lionel Messi beats the rest
he's got skill and lots of grace
he runs across the pitch
with a smile on his face.
Bombing down the left wing
like a bullet from a gun.
When people stop and watch him
they have so much fun.

Jack William Onions (9)
Rufford CE Primary School, Ormskirk

The Farm

A farm is a place were tractors go
All day long they go to and fro
Carting the potatoes back to the farm

In May, the tractor plants the field with potatoes
Then we rely on nature to do its work
The farmer sprays and irrigates the fields
Then the potatoes grow good and strong

When November comes along, the harvester comes out
Busily digging the potatoes out
The engine is roaring, going up and down the field
Collecting the potatoes ready for washing at the farm.

The field is now empty and the potatoes have been sold
The harvester goes on the next field
To start all over again, to keep the potatoes coming in.

Michael Golding (10)
Rufford CE Primary School, Ormskirk

The World Should Be A Better Place

The world should be a better place,
because we would all die.
The news should be less miserable,
like not showing people cry.
The world is too polluted,
by people who can't be bothered to find a bin.
If we all did this, the world would be
less violent, polluted and no longer full of sin.

Matthew Taylor (10)
Rufford CE Primary School, Ormskirk

Ballet Dancer

Ballet dancer, tall and straight.
Ballet dancer, proud.
She dances in the morning.
She dances at night.
She never stops listening to music
Whilst eating breakfast, dinner and tea.
That's because she's a ballerina
Called Victoria Page.

Katie Cottam (9)
Rufford CE Primary School, Ormskirk

Trees

Trees, trees help every day,
They all help us on our way,
We make paper out of them,
But we don't reuse them again and again,
Some of us make trees into homes,
And carve them into shapes,
And some can even make a tree into a pretend chocolate cake.

Joe Skinley (10)
Rufford CE Primary School, Ormskirk

Summer

S ummer smells like melted chocolate ice cream
U mbrellas, throw them away
M ooing of cows eating fresh green grass
M usic of the steel drums
E lephants playing in the mud
R ivers trickling into a waterfall.

Emily Potter (9)
Rufford CE Primary School, Ormskirk

The Robber

One night in an alleyway
a robber crept over to an army base
and stole a tank
and drove to the nearest bank
and bashed through the bank wall.
He stole some gold and he got caught.

Tom Ainscough (9)
Rufford CE Primary School, Ormskirk

Sports

S *plish splash* in the water, swimming in a race
P laying skipping with your best friend
O r playing netball in a team, trying to shoot
R unning as fast as you can, trying to stay in front
T ennis playing with a friend, hitting the ball hard
S o grab a friend and play some sports!

Lauren Shacklady (10)
Rufford CE Primary School, Ormskirk

Friendship

F riendly and calm
R eliable and responsible
I mportant and interesting
E xciting and engaging
N o put down
D oes you a favour
S olves problems with you
H onest and helpful
I nspired by you
P lays with you.

Callum Freeman (8)
St Helen Auckland Primary School, Bishop Auckland

Friendship

F unny and calm
R esponsible and respectful
I ntelligent and important
E xciting and joyful
N o one is a better friend
D ependable
S olves problems
H onest
I nspired
P lays with you.

Matthew Tones (9)
St Helen Auckland Primary School, Bishop Auckland

Friendship

F riends will never split up
R ely on hour friends
I f you play with your friends they will be happier
E njoy playing with your friends at all times
N ever break their hearts
D o not hurt them too much
S ee if they are upset, because if they are, cheer them up
H elp them at all times
I f you're horrible to your friend, she or he will be heartbroken
P lay with all your friends at all times.

Joshua Legg (9)
St Helen Auckland Primary School, Bishop Auckland

The Storm

Black as ravens long since past.
Thunder consuming the darkness and sorrows of thy mind.
Wretched wounds, alas now visible by song alone.
Stand thy ground, armies of silver join the skies in mortal combat.
Whines and whinnies fill the bloodstained heavens above.
Plummet down, deep into the quagmires below.

They're calling once more.

Natasher Devlin (11)
St Hilda's CE Primary School, Manchester

Forever Best Friends

My friend Megan
Is so cool
She is so clever
And does well at school!
Well, my friend Jess
Is so loud
She is such a laugh
And always brings in a crowd!
Megan is sporty
And Jess is naughty!
Sometimes they can be really dumb
No, not really,
But Megan sucks her thumb!
They are both blonde, so am I
We share everything
Especially pie!
We tell each other secrets
And share juicy gos'
But when we fall out
Jess gets extremely cross!
I call Jess, Jessie
And Megan, Pegalino
Megan used to have a cat call Keeno
But I know we will be best friends forever.
We always catch up with the latest trends
And I truly know we will always be friends.

Georgina Easterbrook (10)
St Lawrence CE Primary School, Hurstpierpoint

Cats - Haiku

Cats, cute and furry,
Siamese or tabby cats,
They all love their milk.

Harry Young (10)
St Lawrence CE Primary School, Hurstpierpoint

The Three Hundred - Haikus

The battle begins
Three hundred brave warriors
Ten thousand cowards.

The cowards retreat
Their lifeless bodies fall as
The heroes advance.

Offenders shall die
As blood pours from their death wound
Today all shall die.

As arrows fly forth
The gods are getting angry
And unstoppable

As decades go by
The bloody war will not stop
But then a surprise.

The cowards outflank
Three hundred brave warriors
They know they will die.

Elliot Barton (10)
St Lawrence CE Primary School, Hurstpierpoint

The Stunning Jungle

Baboons engulfed in hair twirled like ballerinas
into the deep, dark jungle.
My sore, tearful eyes adjusted to a poor hedgehog
trapped inside a hole.
Ticklish, irritating raindrops trickled down my soft flesh
and onto the crowded ground.
Teams of leaves gathered together as the moon appeared
from out of nowhere.
My long day has gone and my twenty-four hour long expedition
has ended . . .

Barney Dunnett (9)
St Lawrence CE Primary School, Hurstpierpoint

War Of Fire

War is nature
It will not stop.

It will go to the future
Where lasers will be used
To put the enemies to death
They will blaze and rage

Through cities, villages and towns
We will want to stop

But it is not possible
It will go on and on and on
Until nothing remains
To be destroyed

Only bloody battlefields
And grey skies that watched

The vicious battles
That are still to come
We did not want it
But it had to happen.

James Syms (10)
St Lawrence CE Primary School, Hurstpierpoint

Jungle

Monkeys howl
Wolves growl
Bees drone
Bugs roam

Forest noises surround
Whispers and wails all around
Trees' mutters can be heard
By the biggest tiger to the tiniest bird.

Jonathan Kemp (11)
St Lawrence CE Primary School, Hurstpierpoint

Clock Shop

Clock shop,
Tick tock,
Hypnotic.

Pendulums swing,
Back and forth,
Back and forth,
Counting down to the . . .

Clunk,
Crash!
Tring,
Smash!
Everything shouting simultaneously,
Ear-piercingly harmonious
Song.

Clock shop
Tick tock,
Hypnotic.

Joseph Simpson (11)
St Lawrence CE Primary School, Hurstpierpoint

The Dripping Spear Tunnel Monster

In a dark, damp tunnel
There lived a monster.
It had one red eye
And one very long tie.
It had twenty-seven dripping ears
Teeth like spears
One short arm
Which you think is calm
But it causes alarm.
So when you meet one
You won't have fun,
You'll just run!

Jemima Edwards (8)
St Lawrence CE Primary School, Hurstpierpoint

Marvellous Maths

Maths at school,
It's really, really cool,
5 add 10, 2x3,
Calculate it and you're at ease,
Mean, median, mode and range,
They're really great fun although they sound strange,
Numerator on top, denominator below,
Now you have a fraction, here we go,
Add, subtract, multiply and divide,
People do maths worldwide,
Angles, degrees, measures and time,
Focus on that and you'll be fine,
Even and odd, 2, 4, 6,
They're not all the same, they're match and mix,
Now I've finished my poem,
Listen to me,
Maths at school,
It's really, really cool.

Madeleine Madgwick (10)
St Lawrence CE Primary School, Hurstpierpoint

The Silly Tunnel Monster

It has an arm made out of jelly just like its belly!

Body-blaster
head-slicer
bone-breaker
brain-sucker
skull-cracker
tummy-blower
death-bagger
belly-wobbler
gob-smacker

Beware, it's got a rocket in its pocket!

George Disney (8)
St Lawrence CE Primary School, Hurstpierpoint

Elvis

If you dare to enter the tunnel, brace yourself
for you could come upon an . . .
eye-dribbler,
heart-sizzler,
skin-shredder,
bone-grinder,
eyebrow-plucker,
snot-freezer,
teeth-shatterer,
hair-wetter,
nose scratcher,
feet burner,
Ear-poisoner,
No-bodied,
Rock-feeder,
Low laugher,
Only enter if you're prepared to run as fast
as your little legs will carry you!

Benjamin Lynch (8)
St Lawrence CE Primary School, Hurstpierpoint

Space

Space, space, space
It's such a big place

With its huge stars
That travel so fast

Planets stand their ground
Whilst going round and round

Aliens hide far away
Dashing around in their own little way

Spacemen fly high and high
I guess it's time to say goodbye.

Oliver Towers (11)
St Lawrence CE Primary School, Hurstpierpoint

Boo Boo Poem

Beware, there's a fierce animal in that tunnel
Do not enter.
You might find a . . .
Blood-flooder
Meat-eater
Bone-cracker
Blood-dribbler
Greedy gobbler
Head-ripper
Eye-popper
Dead killer
Head-butter
Multi-monster
Mystery murderer.

This is your last warning . . .

Molly Fullard (8)
St Lawrence CE Primary School, Hurstpierpoint

Space . . . Are You Up There Anywhere?

No sound, nothing there,
No life anywhere,
It's dark, it's cold,
Or so I'm told.
Are you up there . . . anywhere?

No day, no night,
Nothing light,
It's dark all the time,
And it's not a crime.
Are you up there . . . anywhere?

When on Earth, it's dark at night,
I wonder if horrid aliens, fight and fight,
Or is there nothing high above?
Are you up there . . . anywhere?

Holly Spencer (11)
St Lawrence CE Primary School, Hurstpierpoint

There's A Monster In The Tunnel

In a lava-hot tunnel
There was a cylinder-shaped funnel
That led to a . . .

Bone-cracker
Brain-basher
Heart-kicker
Eye-flicker
Face-musher
Feet-stamper
Ear-drummer
Blood-sucker
Clothes shredder

Huge, green, slimy monster!

Harry Forsdick (8)
St Lawrence CE Primary School, Hurstpierpoint

Sphinx

Here is a tale from time to tell
About a monster she is a . . .

Skull scratcher
Bone basher
Heart ripper
Flesh guzzler
Mouth drooler
Claw plunger
Blood sucker
Night creeper
Clothes shredder
She's the . . .
Sphinx!

Nadia Bartlett (8)
St Lawrence CE Primary School, Hurstpierpoint

Cone Collision

White horses canter across the sunlit waves,
crawling up the inhabited caves.
clashing together,
calming the weather,
the sun beams out of the bursting spout.

Slowly starting to whinny and neigh.
the horses chant the sun away,
a gloomy, dark cloud hovers above,
until all life's gone, not a single dove,
coming quickly a cone appears,
making a river of sparkling tears,
all life is gone, all flown away,
no longer is this a happy day!

Bethany Wattam (11)
St Lawrence CE Primary School, Hurstpierpoint

Monster Poem

If you go inside the tunnel you will find a . . .
brain-chewer
poison-spitter
eye-popper
nose-snapper
ear-squeezer
hair-tugger
skull-puncher
tongue-pincher
foot-puller
    and a
tummy-kicker
so don't go in!

Honor Bryant (8)
St Lawrence CE Primary School, Hurstpierpoint

My Teachers!

At my school,
The teachers are cool,
They all are very funny,
And one has a bunny,

Some have dogs,
And some have frogs,
One of them's a nun,
And she always wears a bun,

One owns a fountain,
The other owns a mountain,
All my teachers are very weird,
And each one would love a beard!

Lauren Finch
St Lawrence CE Primary School, Hurstpierpoint

The Gooey, Slimy Tunnel Monster

If you go in a tunnel where nobody goes in at night
But if you go in, you'll meet an . . .

Air-sucker
Water-breather
Ground-shaker
Lung-snatcher
Heart-chopper
Brain-taker
Hair-puller
Stone-thrower
Tongue-twister
Gooey blue monster.

Brandon Haylor (7)
St Lawrence CE Primary School, Hurstpierpoint

The Endless Journey

My heart thumps loudly in the silence of the jungle.
Emerald-green snakes surround me whilst slithering around
up in the high treetops.
Leaves rustling all around, spiders scuttling without a sound.

Ruby-red flowers swaying gracefully, monkeys swooping
high and low.
Scorpions scratch at my feet, branches fall from the luscious
green trees.

I'm surrounded by bugs and animals; I don't know where to go!

The journey has begun!

Megan Burholt (9)
St Lawrence CE Primary School, Hurstpierpoint

Rumble In The Jungle

I jump into the jungle full of awe and wonder!

Slithering snakes echo a *hissss!*
Large lizards leave my sight
So many feelings enter my head.

I jump into the jungle full of awe and wonder!

Red, rosy flowers smell extraordinarily beautiful,
The texture of the palm leaf so smooth yet so mighty
Oh what a beautiful jungle this is!

I jump into the jungle full of awe and wonder!

Reece Piper (9)
St Lawrence CE Primary School, Hurstpierpoint

There's A Jungle Around Me

There's a jungle around me . . .
The light's so dim it's very hard to see, I blame the thick canopy.
The air is warm and there is a very cool breeze.
There's a jungle around me.
Screeches, howls, growls and roars are everywhere.
Monkeys and gibbons flipping from tree to tree with agility.
The air is filled with a terrible scent of fruit and dung.

There's a jungle around me.

David Jackson (8)
St Lawrence CE Primary School, Hurstpierpoint

Rough Sea

Its foamy arms grab out,
as lots of people scream and shout.
White horses toss their silvery manes,
as they gallop across the foaming plains.
Salty spray dances in the air,
then it crashes down without a care.
As it performs, twists and turns,
The angry sea furiously churns . . .

Maya Farlow (11)
St Lawrence CE Primary School, Hurstpierpoint

The Beast

It lurks in caves
Or beneath the sea waves.
It dines upon snakes, worms and eels,
In a day it has at least six meals.
But the beast itself, oh, what a sight!
Just seeing him gives you a fright.
His tail is long, his claws are spiky,
Just waiting for you to scream, 'Oh crikey!'

Rachel Dickinson (10)
St Lawrence CE Primary School, Hurstpierpoint

The Blob

Beware of the tunnel or you might find a . . .
Jaw-snapping,
Eye-zapping,
Bogey-spitting,
Head-hitting,
Teeth-biting,
Knuckle-fighting
Monster!

Joseph Holland-Villa (8)
St Lawrence CE Primary School, Hurstpierpoint

The Poky Tunnel Monster

A monster that flies and keeps in the air
Who is he?

He's poky!
He pokes everybody and does it too
He keeps on spying
Explodes everybody
Gives them a shock.

Joshua Hughes (8)
St Lawrence CE Primary School, Hurstpierpoint

Rainforest Senses Poem

Silvery-grey ruins, scattered with dark green moss
Withering black shadows stalking along walls
Creaking, wooden doors creeping open
Hot, humid sweat creeping down my brow
Bitterly tropical fumes wafting around
Bristling green leaves stabbing into my side.

Lukas Kemp (9)
St Lawrence CE Primary School, Hurstpierpoint

Rainforest Senses Poem

Multicoloured flowers burst open under the golden sun
Shimmering streams glitter like the stars,
Howling monkeys swing from branch to branch,
The scent of a tropical mushroom breathes up my nose,
Fresh air lands on my wet tongue,
Waving palm trees brush against my sweating forehead.

Matilda Jones (9)
St Lawrence CE Primary School, Hurstpierpoint

Silver Sea

Silver fish shining bright
In the dancing blue sea light
Dolphins dive in the crashing waves
While bright fish hide in caves
No more beauty can there be
Than in the graceful, salty sea.

Nina Ince (11)
St Lawrence CE Primary School, Hurstpierpoint

Rainforest Senses Poem

Glittery white dew dropped from the emerald-green leaves
Blue and black spotted dark frogs zipping from tree to tree
Birds singing long, sweet songs
Scented leaves and herbs everywhere
Boiling air evaporated in my mouth
Scorching sun making me sweat.

Reine Tucker (9)
St Lawrence CE Primary School, Hurstpierpoint

Rainforest Senses Poem

Grey dew dripping down red and yellow mushrooms.
Deadly tree frogs as bright as a multicoloured sun.
Shrieks and shrills echoing around.
Sweet scent from wild berries
Unknown tropical herbs on my tongue
Green emerald leaves brushing against me.

Finn Monteith (9)
St Lawrence CE Primary School, Hurstpierpoint

Space!

S pace is big, dark and cold
P lanets hover, new and old
A lways night and never day
C ursing silence echoes away
E arth and space are quite alike,
But I wish it was always a little more bright.

Chloe Wallis (11)
St Lawrence CE Primary School, Hurstpierpoint

Rainforest Senses Poem

Blazing red tree frogs leaping.
Birds swooping and soaring.
Screeching and howling monkeys.
A big red rose, like fire.
Crunchy, hard ants struggling to get free.
Silky, soft leaves beneath my feet.

Alex Moulder (9)
St Lawrence CE Primary School, Hurstpierpoint

Snails

Slithery, slimy snails eat my veg.
They're super-slow,
Their trail is shiny, shimmery, glittering in the golden sun.
Snail shells are my favourite,
They go round and round and round,
So they go all the way back to the beginning again.

Jill Sanger (10)
St Lawrence CE Primary School, Hurstpierpoint

My Jungle Journey

This jungle journey is going to be great.

The canopy over my head only letting a bit of light come through the leaves.
Cheetahs hiding in the trees getting ready to kill their prey.
Noises all around me, monkeys great to watch.

Charlotte Ledger (9)
St Lawrence CE Primary School, Hurstpierpoint

The Sea

Turquoise, tranquil, timid.
Peaceful, poignant, perfect.
Gliding, glistening, glorious.
Winding, whispering, wondrous.
The sea.

Zöe Stevens (11)
St Lawrence CE Primary School, Hurstpierpoint

The Swaying Sea

Splashing, sploshing,
Crashing against the rocks,
Delightfully dancing across the sandy shore.
Whistling waves frightfully fly in every direction,
It's sometimes calm, but it never stops.

Charlotte Burholt (11)
St Lawrence CE Primary School, Hurstpierpoint

The Silent Sea

The sea hugs the sand,
By the jungle lies the sea,
Unknown to anyone,
So tranquil, always beautiful,
Waving goodbye, the sea leaves.

Rebecca Regan (11)
St Lawrence CE Primary School, Hurstpierpoint

Why Me?

Stop this nonsense
I'll give you twenty pence
I've got all the sense . . . so leave me alone

I know I've grown
And I'm not a clone
Don't be the one to throw a stone
Leave me alone

I've got other friends so let's make amends
I don't weigh twenty stone so don't groan
In our group we are not allowed to groan
So let's be friends and give each other pens.

Moritz von Contzen (11)
The British School of Amsterdam, Amsterdam, Holland

Standing On The Roof In The Basement

I'm standing on the roof in the basement
You can't join me but you can
Go wash your hands but keep them dry
Be a woman and a man.

There's a drip from the ceiling that is fixed
Take a seat but stand up
Win that trophy but don't start the race
Have a drink without a cup.

Love the sisters you do not have
Run away from the man who isn't there
Go to sleep but don't close your eyes
Be careless but take care

Answer me but don't say a word
Be silent but be heard
Write a book but forget to write
Don't get into the air but fly quite high

Read a book that was never written
Be happy but be sad
Enjoy my poem and think it's bad
Be the best in class but be bad

Be deaf but hear me
Lose your voice then talk
Walk around without any legs
Do a handstand and walk!

Natalie Schmit (8)
The British School of Amsterdam, Amsterdam, Holland

Summer - Haiku

The smell of flowers,
And the hottest summer breeze,
In the sunset's glow.

Ashling Martin (9)
The British School of Amsterdam, Amsterdam, Holland

What To Do?

This is a poem; it'll get your mind in a mess
But I'm sure you'll like it nevertheless.
So switch on your brain and you won't complain!

Here are a few tips to support here and there,
And soon you'll be too good to compare!

Now start with a title, that's definitely vital,
What kind of verse is guaranteed to immerse?
A haiku, a limerick or a song in reverse!

Have rhymes left and right, now you're a delight.
You'd better watch out, but beyond any doubt,
No need to be fearful, don't cry or be tearful!

What's the theme to be? Happy, cheerful, full of glee?
Or touching and sad to make the reader feel bad?

Whatever you choose, you've got nothing to lose.
Writing is fun, to be proud of when done.
To hang up on the wall, to be admired by us all.

So we're coming to the end, still I have to recommend,
Try not to make it tricky, or try to take the mickey.
You've taken the last leap, now go and fall asleep,
Or go play out in the sun, now all the work is done!

Ben Graham (10)
The British School of Amsterdam, Amsterdam, Holland

Different Dinosaurs

Some dinosaurs are big,
Some dinosaurs wear a wig.

But it is so cool,
That the dinosaurs that rule,

Eat children with dino pyjamas!

Eve Turner (9)
The British School of Amsterdam, Amsterdam, Holland

I Don't Think I'm Quite Human . . .

I don't think I'm quite human.
I think I come from Mars!
My parents own a rocket ship;
They fly it to the stars.

'Cause I have six eyes,
Never tell lies
And plus my sister flies!

I don't think I'm quite human,
I think I come from Venus!
Everybody *must* have seen us!

'Cause we have twelve eyes,
Always tell lies
And our dad is as big as the Bridge of Sighs!

I think I'm definitely human,
I've always come from Earth,
I was a normal person at birth!

'Cause I have two eyes,
Sometimes tell lies,
And none of my family flies or are as
Big as the Bridge of Sighs!

Cassie Howarth-Knight (10)
The British School of Amsterdam, Amsterdam, Holland

My Great Grandmother

In the aeroplane high in the sky,
Eagerly to India, over the clouds I fly,
To see my great grandmother there,
With her kindly eyes and shock of grey hair.

She means more than anyone else to me,
With wrinkly hands she serves me mangoes with cream!
She cooks me tasty, delicious meals,
When I'm with her, how magical it feels!

Together we sit and laugh on our swing,
We watch how a baby bird first moves its wings,
She will be in my mind forever,
Will I forget her? No, never!

She tells me stories she was once told
When she was not quite so old,
Temples bathed in golden sunlight,
Gods and demons having a fierce fight.

I love my great grandmother so much,
When I'm with her I have such
A wonderful time, a wonderful day,
With her forever I will willingly stay.

Lasya Karthikeyan (10)
The British School of Amsterdam, Amsterdam, Holland

Family Complaints

Brother, brother, what is so wrong?
My bulb, it really went *ping-pong!*
You don't mean it had a burst?
I know, I know, it's the very worst!

Bro, Mum, Father, what is so wrong?
Oh no, it went ping-pong!

Mother, Mother, what is so wrong?
My face, it really went *ping-pong!*
You don't mean it had a burst?
I know, I know, it's the very worst!

Bro, Mum, Father, what is so wrong?
Oh no, It went ping-pong!

Father, Father, what is so wrong?
Oh no , the TV, it went *ping-pong!*
You don't mean it had a burst?
I know, I know, it's the very worst!

Bro, Mum, Father, what is so wrong?
Oh no, the TV, it went ping-pong!

Xavier Raychell (8)
The British School of Amsterdam, Amsterdam, Holland

Sword In The Stone

Magical mystery
Crowd pleaser
Royal blade
King predictor
Chosen one

Light source
Truce maker
Peace negotiator
Strength giver
Death decider
Life taker

Power cradle
Strong dwelling
Puzzle mound
Merlin's magic

Eternal glory
New hope
A new king.

Thomas Benjamin Elgar (11)
The British School of Amsterdam, Amsterdam, Holland

What Am I?

Worm picker,
Head turner,
Wing flapper,
Sky soarer,
Mum caller,
Berry eater,
Nest builder,
Song singer,
Cat hater,
Ground pecker.

Isobel Anderson (10)
The British School of Amsterdam, Amsterdam, Holland

Seasons - Haikus

Summer
Vacation is here
Red-hot heating summer sun
Summer's just begun.

Winter

Frozen lake water
People having snowball fights
Winter's just begun.

Spring

Sun's waking the world
Tall trees on a spring morning
Spring has just begun.

Autumn

Crunchy autumn leaves
Gold, yellow, red and orange,
Autumn's just begun.

Sherien Burger (8)
The British School of Amsterdam, Amsterdam, Holland

The Playground

P layful children having fun,
L aughing, chatting, staring at the sun,
A n atmosphere of friendship in the air,
Y es, no, stop, go,
G roups of children happy to share,
R ound and round the children go,
O h! It's nearly time for class,
U tter sadness fills the air,
N o more fun . . . everybody's trying to be last,
D reading lessons in despair.

Kalina Milenova (9)
The British School of Amsterdam, Amsterdam, Holland

My Brother

He's very, very weird
He's unlike most toddlers
He's Mihir the nut!

He's a fighter, *wham*
Punch, kick, push and slam
A kung fu panda fan!

Now he's asleep
Thank goodness for that
But tomorrow's another
Brother attack!

TV's all his eyes can see
And he won't share his time with me

I must warn you now!
If you do enter the house
You may just go crazy
From his cries and shouts!

Shashank Narayan (11)
The British School of Amsterdam, Amsterdam, Holland

My Brother Isn't Human

My brother isn't human,
I don't think he's from Earth.
Now I'm trying to research
How my mother gave him birth.

You may think I'm going mad,
But I think I am right.
If the world does not believe me,
I will get in quite a fight.

If everyone believes me,
All around the globe.
I'll be a millionaire,
And get to buy a new wardrobe.

So my brother isn't human,
He may be from Mars.
I don't know he managed
To fall down from the stars.

Kirsty Graham (9)
The British School of Amsterdam, Amsterdam, Holland

What Am I?

Moon seer
Fire fleer
Meat tearer
Cub carer
Den builder
Human fearer
Day dozer
Night stalker
Eye flasher
Sharp glancer.

A: Cheetah.

Ashley Hill (10)
The Highway Primary School, Orpington

Guess Who?

Sharp stinger,
Great dancer,
Hard worker,
Hexagon lover,
Loud buzzer,
Fast flyer,
Pollen collector,
Flower lover.

A: Honeybee.

Natasha Fenn & Francesca Telling (10)
The Highway Primary School, Orpington

Who Am I?

Nature lover
A closer observer
A world sailor
Evolution maker
Science wonderer
Worm discoverer
Rock collector.

A: Charles Darwin

Danny Hill (9) & Miles Hughes (10)
The Highway Primary School, Orpington

Dolphin - Haiku

Dolphin's eyes filled with
tears as she thinks of the sea,
moves in a small pool.

Scott Simner (10)
The Highway Primary School, Orpington

Dragons

Golden scales glint in the sunlight,
Breath of red-hot flames alight,
Jet black eyes filled with darkness,
Wings spread wide as it takes flight.

White dagger teeth and deadly talons,
Building speed as it soars so high,
A fearsome beast filled with evil,
Or an ancient creature alone and shy?

Rebecca Fryza (10)
The Highway Primary School, Orpington

Music

Boom box blasting
Bass drum bouncing
Beyonce bellowing . . .
Bliss!

Shakira shaking
Spinning, singing
Shimmering the sexy salsa
Super!

Rihanna rapping R & B
Racing round the stage
Roses rocketing through the air
Rock on!

Sarah Louise Davidson (10)
Welbeck Primary School, Newcastle upon Tyne

I Remember

I was with my nana, my mum, my grandad and my dog Max
I was seven
It was at the seaside and we went there in the car
We looked at crabs
We got bars of rock and
I looked at fish
I could smell the water
I could hear dogs barking
We played games on the sand
I could see people running on the beach
I was as happy as a cat playing with a piece of string.

Aimee Cowan (7)
Welbeck Primary School, Newcastle upon Tyne

I Remember

I remember my baby cousin Alfie's christening
I was seven years old
With my family
We were singing songs
The sun was shining
The wind was hiding
I could smell water
I could hear prayers
I could taste cakes
I felt as happy as a hippo in a mud bath.

Charlotte Anne Haigh (8)
Welbeck Primary School, Newcastle upon Tyne

I Remember

I was swimming and splashing
With my dad, brother and sister
We were having fun
The sun was shimmering because it was summer
The wind was blowing and a small breeze made me shiver
I could smell the water on my swimming kit after swimming
I could hear people laughing in the swimming pool
I remember going swimming
I remember it was fun.

Annie Mbikayi (8)
Welbeck Primary School, Newcastle upon Tyne

My Magic Box
(Inspired by 'Magic Box' by Kit Wright)

In my magic box I will put . . .
A picture of my beautiful baby sister and
My cousin's white shiny limousine
A crown and
A red rose from my auntie's garden.

I will put it under my spotty bed and
I will look at it tomorrow.

Tanya Zengenene (8)
Welbeck Primary School, Newcastle upon Tyne

Fiery Wiry

What am I?

Up in your dark den
Breathing fire from your face
Flying with wings of gold
The size of a giant

(I'm a dragon of course).

John-Paul Goossens (7)
Welbeck Primary School, Newcastle upon Tyne

Every Night

Every night I dream a dream of humming birds in spring
Of bright coloured flowers and beautiful butterfly wings

I hear the sound of waterfalls crashing and birds singing
Beyond, a beautiful view catches my eye - a crystal pond

Then I wake and wish that my dream would come true
But it is off to school with my crew
Still wishing and waiting for my dream to come true.

Jamie Brushfield (10)
Welbeck Primary School, Newcastle upon Tyne

I Remember

I remember when me and Mrs Moir got chips
They tasted of vinegar
I jumped on the bouncy castle
I could hear the parrot talking
I could see my dad drinking tea.

Katie Chat (8)
Welbeck Primary School, Newcastle upon Tyne

Rainbow Colours

The rainbow,
the best you'll ever see.
And now, for once
it is sitting over me.

Rainbows lead to treasure,
to silver and even gold.
This one is incomparable
all colourful and bold.

Without rainbow colours,
imagine what life would be.
All dull,
too boring for me to see.

The happiness would be lost,
smiles would be gone.
All dark and gloomy
where the sun once would have shone.

Helen Skingley (10)
West Park Middle School, Worthing

Neptune

The swirling blue planet,
filled with cold liquid
and shiny, moving turquoise oceans.

Frozen cold volcanoes stand still
as fierce winds fly past and white clouds
skim over the darkest section.

As hours pass, swirling clouds pass over
the planet in shadow; as night approaches,
the shiny oceans blink like a turquoise light.

The turquoise planet has shiny moons
following it, as it orbits the sun.

Rian Taylor (11)
Wilton Primary School, Hawick

The Earth

With its beautiful blue seas
and glorious green lands,
it orbits the sun on a tilt.

The rocky crust and molten rock mantle,
with a hard burning core in the middle,
are green and blue
and orange and black.

Whirling dust and misty clouds
and deserts, hot and cold,
seas of water and huge areas of land,
earthquakes and gravity
pulling things down.

The only planet with life,
with plants and trees
and mountains high.

Erin Craig (11)
Wilton Primary School, Hawick

The Sun

This is the hottest star near Earth, it's a big, fiery ball.
This star is always hot and scorching.

The star is a nice, warm, soft planet and it's the biggest star.
This star is our local star.
It's a huge ball of churning, glowing gases.

When it's shining so bright and dazzling,
We cannot see it properly.

There are spots on it.
The spots are in the centre, they are like a big black ball.
Sunspots and patches are very bright with gas.

The core looks like a very big ball,
But it has orange and yellow in it.

Shannon Scott (11)
Wilton Primary School, Hawick

Neptune

A colourful planet
that swirls in space,
that shines brightly.

Colours blend together
to make an icy look
with its wispy blue clouds.

Volcanoes still erupt,
that shoot out cold fountains of ice.

A deserted planet,
eighth from the sun,
with winds that penetrate deep,
gives it its cold atmosphere.

Ella Cairns (11)
Wilton Primary School, Hawick

The Earth

With its ancient volcanoes
and misty clouds, it orbits the sun.

The bursting blue seas and gorgeous green,
it's named the coloured ball.

With deserts burning, hot and cool lands,
its temperature goes up and down.

With whirling winds which whip up dust
and turn into hurricanes.

Its hardy, rocky crust with a core of hard iron,
it's extremely hot.

Mathew King (10)
Wilton Primary School, Hawick

Neptune

A dark, cold, blue planet
Filled with mosaics of wispy clouds.

It seems calm and peaceful
But at the same time, icy-cold and flowing.

A deserted, faraway planet with no light,
Empty, with the strongest winds blowing.

The beautiful shine brightens up the planet
A cold liquid causes the shiny blue.

The cold blue planet has a goddess
Who resembles the sea.

Kirsten Scott (11)
Wilton Primary School, Hawick

Saturn

The orange planet filled with seas of gas
floats on the blue ocean.

Its giant red spot shines through the galaxy
for the planets to see.

Its colourful rings turning from blue to yellow
going round its planets,
surfing its eighteen moons.

The second largest planet and made from liquid and rock,
is as light as the sun and as calm as the moon.
It is truly the best of them all.

Charlotte Dickens (10)
Wilton Primary School, Hawick

Saturn

With its rings of ice all different colours
One of the fastest spinning planets
Is made up of gas and liquid.

Large and round but still light enough to float on water.
It is the second biggest planet.

Made up of a hard rocky core,
Then a thick layer of liquid hydrogen.
Its eighteen moons follow behind, the largest one called Titan.

Sixth planet from the sun with blue, orange and grey
All blending into its brown surface.

Georgia Kirkpatrick (10)
Wilton Primary School, Hawick

The Moon

The cold, calm ball covered in craters,
orbits round the Earth in space.

The rocky, dusty ball of rock
shines in the midnight sky.

This cool, coloured light in the sky
is a satellite of Earth.

The biggest object in the night sky,
it has no light other than the reflection
of the sun.

Madeleine Irvine (10)
Wilton Primary School, Hawick

Venus

A fiery, deadly planet, invaded by gassy clouds,
its rocks bang as the volcanoes erupt loudly.

The green, blue and brown dust,
swirls around its skies as it trembles along the solar system.

The hot air bubbles, sizzling like the sun,
it also spins backwards, burning out the sky.

It can be seen at night in the bright sky
glowing like a star; it whirls everywhere.

Liam Smith (10)
Wilton Primary School, Hawick

Venus

She shines like a brilliant diamond
Brighter than all others around her.

With her mysterious dead volcanoes
She is hot and fiery.

Named after the goddess of love
She is very beautiful.

Also known as the evening star
She shines brightly out of the night sky.

Cristina Antonacci (10)
Wilton Primary School, Hawick

The Sun

A huge, burning ball of gas floating in outer space.
Shimmering on the Earth to make day.
Invisible parts that are cooler than the rest.
Like a bomb in space, the large star burns orange and red.
Flames blast outwards, scorching hot and very bright.
As it sets, the night air cools and its sister comes out.

Shannon Gullen (11)
Wilton Primary School, Hawick

Neptune

A freezing cold planet
with rings made out of ice.

All the blue sea colours
on the surface of the planet.

The solar wind crashing
onto the planet.

The small planet just floats there
nearly crashing into Jupiter.

Connor Smith (10)
Wilton Primary School, Hawick

The Sun

A huge ball of burning gas,
Flames spring out from the surface.

Dark patches of burning fluid,
Like a bomb that does not go out.

Scorching red and orange flames
Flick out and shine upon the dark sky.

Its light floods the universe,
Giving warmth and energy to all.

Kasey Watson (11)
Wilton Primary School, Hawick

The Sun

A giant, burning ball of gas floating in space.

Shining on the Earth to give light in the day;
at night the moon pushes it away till the next day.

Red-hot, fiery flames burst outwards,
like a bomb that never goes out.

This huge, scorching star is like a furnace,
touching anything that comes in range.

Ailsa Nairn (11)
Wilton Primary School, Hawick

The Sun

The burning star shines brightly in the sky.
The star is visible from us on Earth
because it is the nearest star to us.
The dazzling star bubbles and explodes
as lava flies out of the star.
As it glows in the sky,
the ball of gas is slowly dying
as it is halfway through its life.

Michael Smyth (10)
Wilton Primary School, Hawick

Young Writers Information

We hope you have enjoyed reading this book - and that you will continue to enjoy it in the coming years.

If you like reading and writing poetry drop us a line, or give us a call, and we'll send you a free information pack.

Alternatively if you would like to order further copies of this book or any of our other titles, then please give us a call or log onto our website at www.youngwriters.co.uk.

Young Writers Information
Remus House
Coltsfoot Drive
Peterborough
PE2 9JX
(01733) 890066